Savag

(

The Stubbornness of Evil Series 21

Dennis J. Stevens, Ph.D.

About the Author

Dennis J. Stevens, Ph.D. retired from teaching at the

 University of North Carolina Charlotte (UNCC) and is the Director of Justice Writers of America, an organization guiding justice personnel (by invention only) to

articulate their experiences in a confidential setting. Stevens has taught criminal psychology, counselling and justice courses in major universities and counseled high-risk prisoners at Boston, Charlotte, Chicago, and New Orleans. He has published eighteen university textbooks, five popular media books, and nearly one hundred scholarly articles about law enforcement, corrections, and criminology (see crimeprofessor.com). He has led crisis intervention sessions among Boston and New York City officers after 9/11 and the Boston Marathon bombing, New Orleans and Houston officers after Hurricane Katrina, and Chicago and Dallas officers after the

3

execution-style murders of their own. Finally, he has aided in the murder defense of indicted officers, and has developed psychological analysis of both female and male convicted violent offenders in his capacity as a prison treatment provider or group facilitator for the department of corrections in several states and foreign countries. Visit his website at crimeprofessor.com or email dennisstevens503@gmail.com

A Representative List of Books by Dennis J. Stevens

- Struggles of Addicts and Alcoholics Restricted to a Psychiatric Unit, 2nd (2020)
- The Flames of Healthcare and COVID-19 (2020)
- Justice Practitioners and Paranormal Experiences (2020)
- Inside the Mind of the Serial Rapist, 3rd Ed. (2020)
- Toxic Criminal Behavior: Avengers and Copycats (2020)
- Brutal Truths of Young Female Sexual Predators and Ancient Demons (2020)
- Cops At Risk: Health, Homicide, and Litigation (2019)
- City Boys and Girls: Assassins, Predators and Lovers (2019)
- Stories by Sweet Female Offenders Who Will Find You and Dig Your Grave (2019)
- Predatory Nation (2016)
- Criminal Justice and Public Health: MRSA and Other Deadly Pathogens (2015)
- The Failure of the American Prison Complex: Let's Abolish It (2014)
- The Media and Criminal Justice: CSI Effect (2011)
- Wicked Women: A Journey of Super Predators (2011, 2021)
- Introduction to American Policing (2009-2019)

- Police Officer Stress: Sources and Solutions (2008, 2021)
- Community Corrections (2006)
- Community Policing in the 21st Century (2003)
- Case Studies of Community Policing (2003)
- Policing and Community Partnerships (2003)
- Case Studies of Community Policing (2001)
- Measuring Performance: A Guide to Evaluative Research (2001)
- Perspective in Corrections (2000)
- Inside the Mind of the Serial Rapist (2000, 2007)
- Once in David's City (1994)
- The Lyon Sleeps (1991)

Preface

There are believers who reason that evil has to do with angels, spirits, and a deity of sorts. Legendary fables attempt to discredit any truthful investigation about the life flow of evil in all of us. *Savages or Saints: Fake Doctors, Children and Struggles* describe the wickedness of an evil energy that never rests, never goes away, and permanently flows in every human, past, present and future. The peaceful normal-looking image starring back at you from the bathroom mirror reflects a truer representation of a potential criminally violent monster. This book paints a disturbing portrait of all of us keeping a balance between a compassion to savagely commit despicable atrocities against others, versus an attempt to show the world our virtuous ways. We simply await the opportunity or circumstance to violently engage prey sometimes for no reason. No? Think of all the existing struggles such as genocide and warfare over our planet, the violence on American streets by drivers, thugs and some cops, and in classrooms and bedrooms across the nation.

This work reports that some living in central China, move to Hong Kong to hack into organizational websites to falsify credentials as surgeons and are employed by medical centers in Damascus and at war-torn hospitals in Afghanistan and Guatemala. The idea is to calm the buzz in their heads while legally draining the life flow of others. It reports that some children living in abandoned trailer parks, luxurious Manhattan condos, and in Iowa City easily convince others of their innocence with sparkling eyes and honeyed smiles. Then those saints savagely rip into their believers' bodies with little hands, piercing teeth, and a mouth that devours their life fluids without mercy.

Children, even those adapted in New Orleans and Milwaukee are awesome actors, too, mirroring a sweetness while orchestrating the torture and demise of others. Some take years to track down others to provide justice, they say, when the chatter in their head simply wants blood for the sake of blood's sake. For instance, when two soldiers in a war zone raped a child's grandmother and killed her, years later the child, tracked down those soldiers, took a job at the assisted living quarters for wounded soldiers, and raped and killed them with a bat. Children learn how to hack systems for vulnerable prey, how to stalk and kill them, and how to prove their innocence. While other children such as those living in Beverly Hills murder, torture, and drain their victim's body fluids which includes their own teachers, plastic surgeons, nurses, and staff. Murderers are everywhere watching you, and they are rarely apprehended or convicted reports the FBI. Welcome to your graduate level class in Evil 505.

Table of Contents

Chapter 1: Introduction

Introduction

There are believers who reason that evil has to do with angels, spirits, and a deity of sorts. Legendary fables attempt to discredit any truthful investigation about the life flow of evil in all of us. Savages or Saints: Fake Doctors, Children and Struggles describe the wickedness of an evil energy that never rests, never goes away, and permanently flows in every human, past, present and future. The peaceful normal-looking image starring back at you from the bathroom mirror reflects a truer representation of a potential criminally violent monster. This book paints a disturbing portrait of all of us keeping a balance between a compassion to savagely commit despicable atrocities against others, versus an attempt to show the world our virtuous ways. We simply await the opportunity or circumstance to violently engage prey sometimes for no reason. No? Think of all the existing struggles such as genocide and warfare over our planet, the violence on American streets by drivers, thugs and some cops, and in classrooms and bedrooms across the nation.

This work reports that some living in central China, move to Hong Kong to hack into organizational websites to falsify credentials as surgeons and are employed by medical centers in Damascus and at war-torn hospitals in Afghanistan and Guatemala. The idea is to calm the buzz in their heads while legally draining the life flow of others. It reports that some children living in abandoned trailer parks, luxurious Manhattan condos, and in Iowa City easily convince others of their innocence with sparkling eyes and honeyed smiles. Then those saints savagely rip into their believers' bodies with little hands, piercing teeth, and a mouth that devours their life fluids without mercy. Children, even those adapted in New Orleans and Milwaukee are awesome actors, too, mirroring a sweetness while orchestrating the torture and demise of others. Some take years to track down others to provide justice, they say, when the chatter in their head simply wants blood for the sake of blood's sake. For instance, when two soldiers in a war zone raped a child's grandmother and killed her, years later the child, tracked down those soldiers, took a job at the assisted living quarters for wounded soldiers, and raped and killed them with a bat. Children learn how to hack systems for vulnerable prey, how to stalk and kill them, and how to prove their innocence. While other children such as those living in Beverly Hills murder, torture, and drain their victim's body fluids which includes their own teachers, plastic surgeons, nurses, and staff. Murderers are everywhere watching you, and they are rarely apprehended or convicted reports the FBI. Welcome to your graduate level class in Evil 505.

Chapter Flow

The chapter flow consists of three parts extending over ten chapters. After the Introduction chapter, Part I: Fake Doctors consists of Chapter 2 reporting on the early childhood experiences and cyber hunt for prey for Dr. McCarty and Jisel Ruiz. The team learned that hunting prey on line is an art and they efficiently learned their craft of both hacking websites, hacking bored college boys, and for McCarty, pretending to be a physician was easy. Her medical skills were never an issue with anyone including her colleagues. Chapter 3 describes another fake doctor, this surgeon Dr. Mei-hui Cheng, switched places with a real doctor and killed her in Hong Kong.

This fake surgeon became a highly respected orthopedic surgeon in San Jose, California. Chapter 4 begins at Jalalabad Prison in war torn Afghanistan. The chapter ushers readers through Taliban training camps, and Adeela Karza's capture by the Russians, training her as a spy, and bounty collection for her murder of American soldiers under her medical care.

Part II: Fake Children. Chapter 5 particularizes on Morgan who was adapted in Milwaukee, Wisconsin. Her and her girlfriend's youth was reported as living and killing at abandoned trailer parks, and their skillful hacking into organizational computer systems for easy prey. Morgan faked her sexual attack with a soldier who received life in prison without parole. Chapter 6 explains Absinthe's killing field in New York City's Central Park. She believed her killings served God's will. Chapter 7 describes the Russian adaption of Devanna who killed the child of her adapted parents, and was placed in a child detention facility in Iowa. Nothing changed for her, accept her new vulnerable prey.

Part III: Fake struggles. Chapter 8 is about genocide and demonic possession in Guatemala. But underlining it all is sexual slavery, sweet sixteen, and cyber breaches all with the aim of savage attacks. Chapter 9 gets into the dynamic young girl team of the trigger who 'wills' murders and the bullet who commits the murders in New Orleans. Finally, Chapter 10 reveals the young life of Glen from Beverly Hill who savagely dismembers and drains the life fluids of his gender reassignment surgeon, his nurse, and staff. Greta and her wealthy neighbors ganged up and brutally tortured and killed competing gang members as part of their initiation. Eventually, 16 year Greta was arrested, convicted of serial murder, and is serving a life sentence in a high security facility. However, she continued her murder sprees despite her restraints and bit into the bodies of correctional officers and other prisoners. One surveying officer said from his hospital bed, "she's not human." Greta was eventually brutally killed in prison by a correctional officer who was the sister of one of her victims when Greta was on the streets.

When We Think of Serial Killers

We think of torturers, rapists, and serial killers and imagine a crazed drooling monster with maniacal

Charles Manson-like eyes. Most of the individuals in this work had radiant captivating eyes, were sweet, and were lethal with their little hands and their teeth. Often some of my eloquent colleagues such as those at universities and medical organizations attempt to explain the criminally violent behavior of out-of-control creatures as possessing everything from characteristics of antisocial personality disorders (ASP), dependent personality disorders (DPD), and borderline personality disorders (BPD) among other personality defaults. Right, it's not their fault that predators brutally murder, eat their prey's reminds, and drain their body fluids – it's their personality disorder that did it. Are calculating savages compulsive killers or is an evil 'instinct' driving their behavior much like that of an animal?

Some like Richard Gelles, professor and dean of the School of Social Policy & Practice at the University of Pennsylvania, argue that the best indicators of extremely violent behavior is their past violent behavior – no shit! So how do they explain the past violent behavior – daa? Some struggling writers study prisons and report that almost 90% of those criminally violent offenders demonstrated major depressive disorder (MDD). Right, go to the prisons where low level thugs tend to be incarcerated. Could it be that the justice system leading up to his or her actual incarceration had something to do with their personality disorder? Or worst yet, the inexperienced educators and psychologists suggest that those in poverty, and unemployment, and family stressors lead to dangerous behavior. What about wealthy predators such as the wealthy children predators in this book who brutally attack family members, friends, and preschool providers?

Truth of the Matter

Psychopaths who are children including very young children, demonstrate conduct that tends to be cruel and unemotional most of the time, unless he or she is turning on the charm.[1] Chronic life-long cruelty no matter their age, might be born with a predisposition towards violence. Yet, it can be argued that all of us are all born with an evil energy in our bodies to destroy and murder without any feelings toward the victim. Creatures that existed on Planet Earth who are throwbacks to prehistoric beings linked to apes and chimpanzees are not

22

a recent discovery by any means. Nor are the documented facts between the predisposed genetic motivators and mass killings of mankind. Truly those who accomplish the most killings and greatest destruction of mankind are usually geniuses or close to it, or are children. One reason they are not often apprehended is that similar to most chameleons, like Morgan in Chapter 5, she knows how to appear sweet and nonthreatening which of course conceals her real mission – to be blissful and she is very blissful when she destroys others.

Short and Sweet

This will be short and sweet. Alleged experts such as Laurence Steinberg, a professor at Temple University explain why juveniles have little control over their actions and implied criminal actions. "The teenage brain is like a car with a good accelerator but a weak brake," wrote Steinberg. "With powerful impulses under poor control, the likely result is a crash." Based on his findings, the U.S. Supreme Court took into account the growing body of adolescent brain research and banned the death penalty for juveniles. So…. Morgan similar to other juvenile offenders lack control? WTF. Morgan similar to all the predators in this book have very strong control over who and what they are – to be an efficient predator at any age, means calculating skills both physical and mental and great psychological knowledge in selecting their prey. During attacks they are in control. Predators plan, execute, and complete their mission of destruction and death with great precision. They possess the intent, the motive, and the means to destroy and victimize others. Wonder if Larry told the truth about psychopaths, would his gloryhole Temple print his thoughts?

Engage in Persistent Patterns of Behavior

Predators engage in a persistent pattern of behavior that violates the rights of others and disregards both the basic social rules and the basic respect of others which includes their parents or the other way around. That sounds similar to the behavior of most children and frustrated parents. But it also sounds similar to the drivers on our highways – the 'me' driver, right?

A recent study at the University of Michigan confirms that the early signs of psychopathy can be observed in children as young as 2 years old. And even at

24

that young age, those babies demonstrate through their conduct differences in empathy and conscience from other children.[2] How challenging would it be for 'normal' child to fake their absent feelings of love and empathy, and cry whenever the situation merits tears? Perhaps those researchers had not raised children themselves. Roger Miller, the musician and song writer sums it up pretty well, "Some feel the rain, while others just get wet."[3]

For example, combat troops (for God and country), police officers, and correctional officers who have killed others in the line of duty are the good guys? But which army is good and which one is evil? Evil is bad, we're good! It is the natural order of things, and the balance in the universe.

Predators

Some explanations about predators might curl your toes a bit such as, "Predators are stronger, smarter and deadlier than ever before, having genetically upgraded themselves with DNA from other species."[4] The researcher who stated that continues along a realistic approach that predators are always looking for a way to gain an advantage over their prey and "dominate the world where they are hunting."

In Chapter 2, Charlene McCarty and Jisel Ruiz's hunt and assessment of their prey is typical of most predators. Predators are probably the world's most efficient psychological profilers, a thought also expressed my many accomplished criminologists such as Stanton E. Samenow,[5] James Alan Fox and Jack Levin,[6] and Eric W. Hickey.[7] Predators are always on the hunt even when they are praying or laughing. They are always determining vulnerability, and are always engaged in violent criminal activities, yet are always offering the face of innocence and kindness because of their high functioning manipulative skills. Fact is, highly skilled predators could be great Broadway or Hollywood actors.

For most predators including the ones who accounts are in this book, their use of the cyber networks, seeking prey, assessing his potential and actual vulnerability, their methods of tracking their prey before any actual encounter with him or her, and their method of murder are all quite intellectually bound resulting in a very slight chance of apprehension, let alone convicted. Even where and how they killed is ingenious because the possibilities of trace evidence is virtually nonexistent and if it is present, the predator manipulated the crime scene. The FBI reports that their Trace Evidence Unit identifies and compares specific types of trace materials that could be transferred during the commission of a violent crime. These trace materials include human hair, animal hair, textile fibers and fabric, rope, soil, glass, and building materials. What you need to know right now, is that the only thing true about television and movie performances is that they are created as entertainment.

One-Half of all Murders are Never Arrested

The Washington Post reported that out of almost 55,000 homicides in 55 cities over the past decade, one-half of them never ended in an arrest.[8] In fact, the FBI data reports that out almost 15,000 murders, a little more than 6 in 10 ended in an arrest.[9] Of the 8,000 or so persons arrested for murder and nonnegligent manslaughter, only 60 were under 15 years of age, and none were younger than 6. Conviction rates for murder typically run around 4 for every 10 arrested. Know this, predators always possess the intent to kill or rape or to destroy prey. For predatory rapists, they will return and rape the same person again and again until they tire of lack of struggle (most repeat victims stop fighting back), and then they will kill their victim.

Winning a Conviction

Just as a matter of understanding, for a prosecutor to earn a guilty verdict, he or she must bring evidence to three elements: the country of Los Angeles reports that: "Crimes can be broken down into elements, which the prosecution must prove beyond a reasonable doubt. Criminal elements are set forth in criminal statutes, or cases in jurisdictions that allow for common-law crimes. With exceptions, every crime has at least three elements: a criminal act, also called *actus-reus* (Latin term); a criminal intent, also called *mens-rea* (also a Latin term); and concurrence of the two. The term conduct is often used to reflect the criminal act and intent elements. As the Model Penal Code explains, "'conduct' means an action or omission and its accompanying state of mind" (Model Penal Code § 1.13(5)."[10] Most often motive, opportunity, and means or MOM are the elements a prosecution must prove beyond a reasonable doubt that leads to a conviction.[11] Yes, the characters in the book exercise all three elements of the criminal act, the criminal intent, and concurrence of the two. But the bridge is that inspectors might not live long enough or keep the job long enough, or become apprehensive in identifying a predator who might attack an investigator's family members or be one of the family members.

Part 1: Fake Doctors
Chapter 2: Dr. Charlene McCarty and Jisel Ruiz and the Prison Treatment Provider

Overview

Twenty-six year old Charlene McCarty, MD owned Glamour Medical Spa located in Wilmington,

North Carolina and was questioned (not arrested) by federal agents. Her offices were invited by federal agents dressed in protective gear. They seized McCarty's documents and files which after close investigation never revealed a breath of federal healthcare fraud. She promoted a treatment as a practicing physician for first responders, healthcare providers, and the public willing to pay her price for treatment. She advertised vitamin C infusions to treat COVID-19 patients. Prior to that

COVID-19 treatment, she promoted the vitamin C infusions to treat (H1N1) pdm09.

Linked Website to Various Local and Federal Agencies

A dark shadow would be arriving over many organizational websites as McCarty efficiently linked her website to several news' agencies, Johns Hopkins University research sites, the federal website consisting of in particular Centers for Disease Control and Prevention (CDC), WebMD sites, and both county and state medical warning and recommendation sites devoted to COVID-19 news and reports. She made personal presentations to both Georgia and North Carolina governors who then recommended her to their state's first responders at several jurisdictions and healthcare personnel at several hospitals. She made personal presentations at many agencies and of course, numerous anxious personnel at those agencies purchased her vitamin C infusions. They purchased the first round during the presentation and received their products and also paid for the second round and third round which would be mailed to them in 90 days and 120 days. After each presentation she would always end it with, "You'll will be supercharged to night so be gentle," followed by a huge grin which jumped across her girlish face.

Obviously, she was highly skilled with cyber dynamics and needless to say, she was making huge profits from her efforts which were primarily promoted through online videos and through her personal presentations. Officials treated her as though she were a goddess not just because of her knowledge linked to treatment and computers, but also because of her pretty girlish grin, her very cute way of walking, and her imitation of Donald Duck's voice.

FBI Spokesperson

An FBI spokesperson said that the "Investigation includes allegations that the (Glamour Medical Spa) clinic provided fraudulent treatments for COVID-19 and that the clinic did not observe proper protocols to protect staff."[12] Nonetheless, federal investigators could not gather any sufficient evidence that even hinted that federal impropriates existed. Also, federal investigators could not uncover any evidence that federal regulations or laws were even approached by McCarty.

McCarty's Intelligence and Skills

A point of interest is that Charlene McCarty (as was Jisel Ruiz her new partner in crime, see below) is highly intelligent and an ingenious learner who taught herself how to master the cyberworld. Her intention was to create an identity including the credentials that she was a medical doctor (MD). Her computer skills helped sell her services, and it lured her and her partner's prey into vulnerable circumstances. She searched the internet for COVID-19 remedies, and taught herself about the deeps of medication. She developed a website containing her recommendations, her picture and a picture of her clinic, too. Also, some images of allegedly happy patients were seen on her websites.

It's remarkable that McCarty's only friend, Jisel Ruiz (see below) were both wicked bright and highly manipulative, loners in that they would never go to concerts, the movies, and never dated. In fact they both loathed males: they didn't trust them, didn't enjoy their presence, and seriously hated them enough to lure them through their cyberpredator skills to 'qualify' over 40 young men for murder (details below). Both Charlene and Jisel were brilliant, computer and website savvy, and highly motived to crush as many males as possible and at the same time, push out those cute innocent smiles to alter any thoughts that they were the perpetrators of any unlawful behavior including speeding. Their mutual rationale about males could be found in Jisel's comment to Charlene during a prison treatment visit (details below), "They all think with a certain part of their anatomy, and their only goal is to get off." Both of their early childhood and adult life for that matter fit one overview profile: they always possessed the intent of criminal behavior and thought a great deal about the suffering of victims because that was one motivator towards murder.

North Carolina Conviction

Eventually, the State of North Carolina prosecuted McCarty as a favor to the feds and won a conviction of sorts. It was well documented that the North Carolina Women's

Prison had become the site of a major COVID-19 outbreak,[13] and it was argued by McCarty's defense team that incarceration at a North Carolina prison she could do good there with her knowledge and skills. For Charlene (with the hat on and her hair down, and Jisel whose fingers are on the computer), it meant a new audience of her medical products and skills. Drug traders possess a similar attitude about incarceration – captured new buyers.

North Carolina's department of correctional services sent her to Swannanoa Correctional Center for Women located at Black Mountain, North Carolina as opposed to a local jail which typically housed defendants for sentences of less than 6 weeks. Charlene sentence consisted of 4 weeks, and some thought she was considered a high risk to other prisoners, but that was not her official security level probably because of her intake assessment officer - Jisel.

Jisel Ruiz the Prisoner Assessor

Before Charlene similar to all prisoners, a typical prisoner intake process was conducted. Her prison assessor or evaluator was Jisel Ruiz (more about her below), who would also visit Charlene several times every week at Black Mountain which was not a common occurrence among assessors with prisoners.

Once Charlene McCarty was released, she knew Jisel lived in Charlotte, North Carolina. She went home to Wilmington, packed her personal belongings, what was left of her professional files, her medical (fake) doctor's degree and license despite the state's withdrawal of her license, and moved in with Jisel. Charlene explained their relationship this way: "I trusted her with my life and my body and hopefully, we would become better lovers," (implying that they were involved intimately to some extend or another with each other during Jisel's prison visits).

Storyline Resources

For a reader's close look Charlene McCarty and Jisel Ruiz, the collaborations between them are at the core of their stories in this book. Also, Jisel's mother, official records, and some of their (living) victims, at least the ones who escaped murder contributed to their storyline, too. Charlene kept journal type notes while in a prison treatment group and continued those notes after her release outlining her accomplishments cored in her playful appetite. Her journal is currently in the possession of a confidential source.

Charlene McCarty Early Experiences

Charlene McCarty an early June baby, was raised in Dalton, Georgia and graduated as the valedictorian from Dalton High School. The McCarty's family consisted of three girls: Emma or 'M,' Cerise or 'Ressi,' the baby Charlene, and one amazing little dog, Happy. The family attended a community church every Sunday, and the children attended bible class even after Nat McCarty their father left the family home primarily because of Charlene's behavior and his wife and other daughters who criticized Nat when he disciplined Charlene. "She's only a baby." Charlene was very prolific at resisting various passages from the Bible with the face of angel at the same time she was plotting her next round of foul behavior.

Evolution of Wicked Evil Behavior

Nonetheless, Charlene's evolution of evil was characterized in the shadows of her conduct at age 4. For instance, her English cocker spaniel puppy, Happy, was show-groomed and very playful, in fact too playful for Charlene. In the back yard, she held Happy by the throat and squeezed several times allowing Happy to grab some air fascinating her to no end. Finally, she learned that when she twisted Happy's neck and kept pressure on it, Happy died. She wrapped it in a towel and dumped Happy in the family's garbage container.

Her father moved out of the family home because of Charlene's continual harassment and her manipulation of her mother and two older sisters into believing that Charlene, with Charlene's insinuations that he was sexually abusive towards her. For instance, Charlene hatred her father so much that at age 6 he thought they were playing when she slapped him and dropped a "Boston pancake" (pooped on him) on his chest. She screamed for the attention of her sisters who jumped in and pulled them apart. Charlene blamed him for her lack of control by attempting to "do something stupid to my bottom," and "he pushed in on my tummy and laughed at me."

Charlene often spied and attacked her older sisters. For instance, when Charlene was 7 years old and

Ressi her favorite sister was 12, she attacked Ressi a wet mop and throw out her imitation of Donald Duck which she enhanced through her teenaged years. Other times, Charlene entered the restroom while Ressi sat on the toilet. Ressi knew better than to demand Charlene's exist or tell mom about Charlene's behavior because attacks would become intensified as M learned (M left home for a private high school and eventually college primarily to stay away from Charlene). Ressi felt sorry for her little sister because it appeared that she had no issues or regrets about her behavior.

Charlene cleaned Ressi after she was finished and proceeded to insert her fingers, tooth brush, and anything else in the bathroom that would fit inside Ressi's private parts, mouth, and between her toes. All the while, Charlene would talk about whatever, and her voice was always high pitched even when she was a baby – she never cried.

In a way, Charlene's behavior from her early childhood through adulthood implied that she did not possess a moral compass or put another way, no borders.

Education and Visit to an Old High School Teacher

After graduating high school, Charlene attended Emory University and Emory University School of Medicine in Atlanta, Georgia on full scholarships. She graduated as a nurse. Yet, she cyberhacked the school's record, and entered various medical courses that applied to an MD graduate after her name. She provided grades for her graduate courses largely consisting of 4.0 on a 4.0 system.

Once she established her business in Wilmington, she visited her favorite high school teacher at Dayton High School. Randal Jesse Davidson, whom she loved to harass and loved watching his stupid behavior when she played with his mind. This time, in her best Donald Duck imitation, she convinced him to fire his 22 pistol out his school's office window into the field below.[14] Then she proceeded to convince him that he had killed someone and should turn himself in to the police. The bullet never hit anyone, but the incident caused a full-scale lockdown until Davidson, 53, was taken into custody by the SWAT team.

Jisel Ruiz Early Experiences

Jisel was born on Christmas day in Columbia, South Carolina to the proud parents of five daughters, all older than Jisel but she reminded the cutest of all the girls with her constant smiles and happy eyes right up through her adulthood. Her daddy was the assistant attorney general for the state of South Carolina and the governor's right hand man despite that both Jisel's mother and father were born in Mazatlán, Mexico which is on Bay of California, west coast. The Ruiz family lived in the Forest Acres neighborhood an upscale community in Columbia, South Carolina. None of their siblings including Jisel ever went without – that is, they were all spoiled children and would be the rest of their lives. Jisel was probably the worst of the lot not just because she was the youngest but also because she possessed a high pitched voice that seemed to demand attention.

When Jisel was 5 years old, she attempted to catch her father off guard by grabbing his penis through his swim suit while at the lake on a family picnic. She let out her high pitched voice in terror, despite the obvious that she was the perpetrator of that action. That was the beginning of her stubbornness of evil conduct that veiled her darkness without ever a glimmer of light. She loved music and often bounced around the house to the tunes of the day. Her favorite singers were Lady Gaga and Taylor Swift, and when she heard them her favorite artists, her brain stopped whatever it was doing, a chill reached over her back down to her legs, and she danced and danced without a care in the world.

Before 4th Grade

Before Jisel reached 4th grade, she got her 7th grade sister so sexually excited that her sister proceeded to force herself upon Jisel (when in fact, Jisel had done the luring). These two incidents – initiating sexual relationships until her victim responded, reoccurred over her young life and adult life many times with different victims. Other incidents included her theft from retail stores consisting of candy, and later clothes from Aéropostale and similar establishments. It is likely that often the merchants were aware of her theft, but remained quiet until they would see her mother or sisters. More than once, Jisel revealed that after using the retail establishment's rest room, she would wipe herself with hanging clothes in the store. Sometimes she would return to see if anyone tried on her improvised toilet paper.

Private Schools

All of Ruiz girls attended private schools from early daycare through high school. Jisel and her two twin sisters attended Wake Young Women's Leadership Academy in Raleigh through 8 grade and Salem Academy High School, at Winston Salem, NC. Both schools were all females as were their teachers and gym instructors. Through high school, the sisters lived together in an Academy dorm. One of the twins, wanted to attend a public school but both Jisel the shortest and youngest, and Juana decided to take matters in their own hands to keep Alejandra at Salem Academy. Their reasoning was that the three girls were inseparable, and resided in the same Academy dorm room. If Alejandra left, another girl not necessarily of their choice, would be assigned Alejandra's bed and that wasn't going to happen. After long tearful conversations, and hugs, Jisel grabbed her older sister's jaw, stuffed her fingers along Alejandra's gums, and said while their eyes were centered upon each other, "You are never going to leave me and Juana, got it?"

"Okay. But I hate it here." The two sisters threw her on the bed and literally raped her through tears, frantic motions, and hard sequences. In fact, two more times while in high school, both Jisel and Juana had to repeat their foul behavior to keep Alejandra "on the straight and narrow." Jisel was always the aggressor of those punishments even though she was younger than her the twins.

Jisel was rigid in her feelings toward her long-legged sisters. Juana and her often held each other all night long and every so often glanced at Alejandra who quickly closed her eyes pretending to be asleep.

"Jealous?"

"No, no," Alejandra replied.

"You can't join us cuz you're still a baby," announced Jisel.

Jisel implied that between her and Alejandra, "heavy animosity existed" for Jisel. "She was not to be trusted, but Juana was like my little sister." Whatever that meant is still undetermined.

Jisel Ruiz and Professional Credentials

After high school, Jisel decided to attend MIT in Boston, and of course they couldn't refuse because of her 4.0 grades from Salem Academy and her family's financial contributions and political connections. Her undergraduate work was in psychology, and once graduating with another 4.0 grade point average, she attended Northeastern University also in Boston and worked on her counseling degree and eventually became an accredited cognitive behavioral psychotherapist. She returned to the south but this time took a condo in downtown Charlotte, North Carolina and passed her the state's certification in counseling.

The Department of Corrections hired her as an intake evaluator and one of her earliest evaluations was Charlene McCarty whom was immediately attached to her.

Charlene McCarty and Jisel Ruiz Luring of Young Men

As you already know, Charlene and Jisel became roommates and partners in murder motivated by the mutual thought of venturing out to "make things right."

45

They developed a website together to attract vulnerable university male students from UNC-Charlotte, Queens University and Davidson College.

Their first priority was never to use their own internet service in their condo to lure young men to various locations. They would travel to Starbucks, Showmars, and public and school libraries among others and use their internet services. One computer of the girls was used to design websites, another was utilized on the social media platforms to obtain information about available girls and desperate boys, another computer was used to commutate with their potential victims, and yet another was their personal computer never to be part of their cybercrimes. They may have used more computers in their cyber activities, but the ones mentioned were the ones known.

 They downloaded pictures of pretty young girls from public domains, Facebook, Instagram, Snapchat, Tumblr, Skout, Hinge, and Tinder among others. They edited those images

46

by resetting, cropping, adding artistic effects, and changing backgrounds. They changed the color of hair, the color of eyes, and the narrowness of chins. For example, this image was copied from public domain and edited using the tools available at the website. For instance, the caption used under the above image was: "I'd love to ride in cars." They used those images to attract young men who would be valnerable enough to submit to the predators.

Bored College Students

Online, they would start a cyber conversation with a 'bored college student' looking for someone to "get me through" the day or night or class. If a respondent appeared to be proficient at sports or physically fit, that is an athlete of sorts, he was immediatey informed that 'the girl' found her 'knight' and if that didn't work out, she'd be back looking for him. He was also deleted from the conversations and blocked.

By the Numbers

By their own count, it usually took 20 respondents to their web queries (some "were obvisiouly police offiers, girls, young boys suddenly frigthened off, or teachers, or just "cyberjerks," wrote Charlene):

- 8 would continue the cyberconversation
- 5 asked for more photos of the bored coed (if they asked for nude photos they knew the person at the other end of the message was probably a cop or a studpid male (sometimes Charlene or Jisel would ask, "So what ya'gon'a do with my picture?"
- 3 actually wanted to met her
- 2 showed at the disinated location which changed during the traveling process via markers left at each supposed meeting location
- 1 was permited a meeting

These predators understood the statistics of vulnerable and available victims, which is a common understanding of most predators. It's about the numbers!

Hunting Victims is an Art

The girls would always research their prey at various websites, and through university photos and

Google images among other websites. They would always ask the boy what high school he graduated promting more research about his authenticity as well as the name of his best friend or favorite professor. Often if there was a hit of suspiction about the boy or they just wantd to troll the campuses, they would wear their college outfits, grab their cells, and head out to one of the campuses. They would snap photos, and blend in with campus students. This photo shows Charlene far left on her cell wearing a red wig while Jiset snapped this imagine. The potential victim is the boy wearing the Kent University sweat short in front of the dark haried girl, yet they both are students at the University of North Carolina-Charlotte (UNCC). In this case, the predators decided to kill both the dark haired girl holding their potential victim's hand at the Blue Ridge Mountains in North Carolina after luring them there with a photoshoot for Niner Times, UNCC's newpaper. The murder of the couple was exciting raising the emotions of both predators. They sexually played with the boy infront of his girlfriend who cried and cried until Jisel smacked her. Then they played with her all the time allowing him to watch. Their victims both struggled and tried to get out of their handcuffs and ankle restraints without any luck.

"I'm so stoked that we brought those Peerless cuffs from Amazon.com," said Jisel and added, "Good call, girlfirend. They can try all they want."

Plans of Cyberpredators before the Outing

Charlene McCarty and Jisel Ruiz were extraordinary cyberpredators. These predators as you have already learned had an amazing method to hunt prey. But they also had a scheme of killing an unsuspecting victim, a method of disposing the prey's body, clothes, and eliminating any potential evidence left at the crime scenes. For one, if they murdered a victim at the Blue Ridge Mountains in North Carolina, they would plan their next "outing" (that's what the girls called it), at the Appalachian Mountains in Virginia. Of course, a different victim's college location also played into their outings, and during the spring months, outings didn't happen because of the many people hiking through the mountains.

Body Tactics

Both predators before an outing, braided their hair in a tucked fishtail braid, so that none of their hair was hanging. They never wore perfume, deodorant or jewelry including rings. Their nails were short, and they never planned outings around their menstrual cycles. Charlene was not a heavy bleeder, but Jisel was and it was painful for her, too.

The plan was that one of them entered shallow but rapid running water ways close to shore in the mountains of North Carolina, South Carolina, and Virginia, while the other hid on the shore awaiting him. Their prey was advised about the time and location of the 'girl' who hoped to meet him. Both wore a cute seamless sport bra and a revealing thong (not just to lure her victim but because the less clothing, the less likely evidence could found by investigators).

After Victim Appeared

The girl hiding alerted the other girl standing knee deep in the waterway of his presence by holding up a branch. By the way, only once had Jisel encountered a park ranger while in the water. She told him that she was so taken by the water that she had to take a dip. "I'm sorry, officer. Am I bad?" Another time while Charlene was in the water, two hikers passed by. She pitched, "Dad, is that you, I don't have my contacts on?" One of the hikers, replied, "Sorry. Thought you were somebody else," and continued their hike.

Smooth Operators

Once their victim appeared, the girl in the waterway appeared overly excited and called out to him from the water, "I hope you came to save me," was a typical first comment. She prompted him into the water, "Take off your shoes and clothes if you want," which usually bought the boy into the water. As he approached with hands waving to keep his balance, her accomplice would jump on his back and would pull his ears. They rode him, one suggested, "as though we're rodeo stars." Both predators kept his head submerged until he stopped moving. They would never drag his lifeless body to shore, but often played with his head, pretending that his mouth was moving up and down while the words from one of his killers blurred out which somehow excited both predators. Charlene did fine imitations of Donald

Duck and they both laughed sometimes to tears. The murder was always an exciting moment for both girls.

Sometimes, they would pull on his penis to see if he screamed. "No it doesn't hurt? You're a big boy," Charlene might say in her Donald Duck voice or something similar to this comment as the boy floated on his lifeless back. His killers had thought of grilling parts of his body, but the smoke would mark their location. Sometimes they might push his body further out into the water after covering it with branches of leaves. Not to hide him, mind you, but to confuse investigators.

Smiley Face Killer

A social media article profiled what it called the Smiley Face Killer, who supposedly was a nameless serial killer, who continued to be at large, and allegedly responsible for over 40 drowning deaths of young college male students attending local colleges near Charlotte.[15] Hard evidence, the article stated, about the Smiley Face Killer is nonexistent, but the theory has serious adherents. They choice the nick name because of the smiley face graffiti often found near several places where they believed the deceased were murdered. "If true, the Smiley

Face Killer could be the most prolific — and therefore most dangerous — active serial killer in 2020," wrote Pauli Poisuo. Critics of the "Smiley Face Killer" theory suggest that the victims were most likely binge-drinking and drowned accidentally, and point out that smiley face graffiti is absurdly common in basically any city. Nonetheless, apparently, investigators continued to believe that the killer was a young male and a student at a local college. Often, police and FBI investigators were on various campuses talking to the guys, and when our girls saw them, they did everything in their power not to laugh. Our predators were never apprehended let alone suspected of those crimes.

Update

Charlene McCarty and Jisel Ruiz murdered bored university students for pleasure. Some might say that women whom characterize a malice and evil existence can twist them into the "completely incomprehensible — female serial killers who show the darkness possible inside a human being."[16] Such is the case of Charlene McCarty and Jisel Ruiz who from birth held onto a flame of merciless murder. Both were prosecuted for first degree murder and received a life sentence, with no possibilities of parole. However, McCarty was released after five years of some strange reason, and the following day was implicated in double homicide of a couple hours before they were to take their wedding vows. She said that the almost bride had no business getting married and intervened prior to the ceremony. The father of the almost bride who was in the next room killed McCarthy with his bare hands and was never prosecuted at the suggestion of the AG's office.

Jisel Ruiz was also prosecuted and convicted of 1st degree murder. She was sentenced to life in prison without the possibility of parole. She died in prison a few months after her incarceration by a correctional officer who reported that Ruiz was protecting the 16 year old prisoner who wanted to bring charges against the officer for brutal rape while in her locked down cell. No charges were brought forward against the officer but the word is that the officer continued to rape the 16 year prisoner. The officer sometimes invited her colleagues to also have sex and torture the prisoner. Apparently, the officer was feared by other personnel so much so that no one interfered with her rapes not only of this 16 year but other prisoners, too.

Chapter 3: Dr. Mei-hui Cheng is Gokarmo Zhaxi in Hong Kong and San Jose, California

Overview of Stolen Identity

Dr. Mei-hui Cheng turned out to be Gokarmo Zhaxi (meaning prosperity) who was from rural Jiaju Tibetan Village, Danba, Sichuan Province in China.[17] Zhaxi prefers the nickname Zha and was skilled at murdering visiting students to her village and eventually felt it was time to leave for Hong Kong and eventually America. Language wasn't a problem since Zha spoke English and Sichuanese, which is a dialect of Mandarin, the common language of China and Cheng's native language, too. Zha took Cheng's identity, property, and her surgeon internist position at Li Ka Shing Faculty of Medicine of the University of Hong Kong. Zha had no medical experience, yet was applauded by her colleagues and honored several times by the hospital before accepting a chief surgeon's position at Forest Surgery Center in San Jose, California. Her new husband went to work in private practice for an old medical school colleague in Sana Clara about a 15 minute drive from their castle like home in the Almaden Valley in San Jose. Dr. Cheng had to Uber to work because she didn't like to drive, and had no sense of direction.

Zha's Hometown

Jiaju Tibetan Village, Danba, Sichuan Province is considered a "Tibetan Fairyland" by tourist agents but Zha didn't see that way. If she never saw another panda, she might be the happiest girl in the world. The village is comprised of 140 Tibetan homes, each with a distinctive crown-shaped roof, red eaves and white walls.[18] Winding brooks are scattered everywhere resembling pieces of a chessboard, with the occasional kitchen chimney puffing smoke up from a wood fire. Apple and pear groves are everywhere. Emerald terraced fields stand in stark contrast to severe mountain heights and white snow peaks. Despite her the beauty of her hometown village, she couldn't wait to jump on a bus for Hong Kong when she 13 years old.

Cheng's Personality

The 'new' Cheng had a pleasant personality, was very

 professional and knowledgeable, with a submission style of manipulation. She was up, friendly, and nonjudgmental. She was also tall for a Tibetan Chinese girl, but easily could pass as male

depending on her clothing. Needless to say, she was exceptionally bright, never spoke unless she knew how her words would be perceived by her listener. She always thought through how others would interpreted her conduct, words, and ideas. Some might say that she read their minds, but in truth, this Tibetan Chinese girl knew how to make Einstein blush and Genghis Khan tremble. At birth, she was not born alone, and she recognized those demons in her spirit whispered to her every moment of her life without compromising their objectives.

Buddhism and Zha

Zha's clan were Buddhist, but Zha only accepted the Buddhist mandates when it was reasoned to fulfill her

59

destiny – taking the light out of living things. Just as a matter of understanding, the basic doctrines of Buddhism include the four noble truths: existence is suffering (dukhka), suffering has a cause (trishna), there is a cessation of suffering, which is nirvana, and there is a path to the cessation of suffering.[19] In essence, independent life styles were never part of Buddhism and that tradition in and by itself was one reason Zha rejected Buddhist philosophy. She interrupted the noble truths as the suffering of others whereby she administered that suffering to those others which would bring her closer to nirvana. When she turned Buddhism upside down to comply with the whispers from the spirits in her head bringing her a comfort in appeasing her demons. Obviously her thinking process was far different from other Buddhist youngsters and adults.

Young Zha and Imaging Murder

Zha knew she was different from the other children in her village, and she recognized that she was different from the students visiting her village from other parts of China, Japan, the UK, and the U.S. She was alone as her parents worked the fields and traveled the country side for several days at a time. She had no siblings or other family members monitoring her whereabouts although her parents thought she was learning the traditions of their family. She attended school to learn English and a few other topics but only when it enhanced her plans of leaving the village.

When she was probably 8 or 9, she's not sure, she slid into a closet in student's visitor room in Jiaju. A European young boy pulled her from the closet, and pitched her to the floor. As he kneed over her, yelling at her in his country's language, she reached up to defend herself. Her little hands were on his chin and slid down his neck. She never panicked and didn't then nor was she frightened. She had few emotions but was in the process of learning a new chilling emotion – the trill of physically dominating another person. She felt the spirits were pushing in on her hands around his throat even though she was on the bottom. Her thoughts carried her to her eyes which would accept the melt down of her victim's eyes. She was ready to act, but another student opened his door and pulled him off of her. She ran as fast as her legs would take her through the door.

From that experience, she practiced on her on face, toughing, squeezing, and slapping herself. She learned that a weak spot on her throat was, she would learn a few years later was called the larynx. The experience of fingering her larynx brought her a little pleasure, too. If she were European, she would have said "sweet," but *xìng fú* (in Mandarin) explained her happy thoughts at the moment.

One way she built strength in her hands was to swing the local cats and little dogs in the air by their tails. She then turned her 'training' on street dogs which were running wild all over the Sichuan Province. It took four of five attempts to kill her first dog because she had to learn to keep her face away from the animal's teeth and to attack the animal from the back as opposed to the front of the dog.

Over the following months, she practiced on squeezing the larynx of dogs and children but couldn't find the larynx on chickens. She kept mental notes and one of the most extravagate notes was her sensational feeling that run through her body almost like a cool breeze when she accomplished her mission – to end the life of a living thing at the end of her little fingers.

Zha's Killing Field

Zha stood across the street in her Jiaju Tibetan Village from the tourist quarters watching students leave and enter. When she spotted a student a little bigger than her, she entered her room from the street since the dorms were an open floor facility similar to most homes and buildings in Sichuan province, she made plans. She took inventory of the student's western clothes some of which she folded and placed at the door.

This time, 10 year old Zha didn't hide in the closet in the visiting student's guest room. She sat on the bed in the dark waiting. When the student opened the guest room door, she probably asked Zha what she was doing there. Zha jumped from the bed, and jumped on the student's back as she closed the door. Her little fingers found the larynx of her prey. Seconds later the student was on the floor with Zha's fingers tightly wrapped around her. But the student pushed her off, and Zha went flying, hitting the wall. Zha didn't panic. She approached the student again. This time, the student died quickly and

Zha's smile and happy spirit blanketed the room. She took her time packing the student's stuff into the backpack of the student after dumping her books to the floor. Much to Zha's surprise, the student's computer and cell were in a compartment of the bag. Of course, she had few ideas on how to use them, but would learn. It was as though she were in a candy store, she was ready to enter the room next door but decided to gather her valuable treasures and leave. She felt no guilt or emotion in taking items that belonged to someone else just as she had no guilt or remorse for taking a life, but her emotion for taking the life was totally amazing. She was pleased with herself because life's treasures and spirits were to be shared, said Buddha or at least that is what she believed.

Visiting Starbucks

Zha visited a Starbucks a few miles from her home, of all places and chatted with other students of various ages.[20] Because of her pleasant personality, her submission style of manipulation, finding mentors and friends or victims was an easy and welcomed experience. Little had any of those new friends suspected that she was a talented predator enhancing her knowledge, her inventory, and her enhanced knowledge of potential victims. Some invited her to their dorms and homes. A few boys had a different interest in Zha when they invited her to their student rooms. With the first boy, because of her curiosity, he tried to complete his sexual attack of her, but had an early ejaculation and never penetrated her. She simply left the room without a thought. The other boy, she killed, not because of the attack but because he was vulnerable, and she couldn't help her appetite which shouted to her – feed me. Killing had greater benefits than sexual outcomes, she realized some time ago.

Mastered Her Craft

At 14 years of age, Zha had mastered her craft – extinguishing the life spirit of a living creature. Again sitting on the bed of another student she attacked her from the back much like killing dogs. There was no lost time in the kill. Zha had taken inventory of the student's possessions and had her clothes, identification, a bus ticket, and other items ready for her departure. The dead student was on the floor, so Zha picked her up, took off her clothes, dressed her in her pajamas, and laid her in bed. She experienced no sensation from her victim's body when she felt her and that didn't surprise her because her 'light' and spirit were helping her victims to suffer as she understood Buddhism. Her victim had a stuffed animal next to her bed, so Zha knowing a little about western behavior, put the little animal in bed with her victim. On the nightstand was a yellow bottle of pills which Zha could not read but took all the pills out of the bottle and shoved them into the mouth of her victim. She worked the victim's chin and throat with the mission in mind of her swallowing all of the pills. Her thoughts were that any investigation of her victim's demise would end in suicide, something she learned from the students at Starbucks, at least the boys who attempted to impress her with their knowledge.

Getting Out of Town

The authorities near Zha's hometown were examining many homicides in the providence.[21] Seems murder went wholesale. Chinese prosecutors indicted 40 of Shisun's village residents for arranging 17 murders. At least 35 more deaths were under investigation; it was concluded that dozens more would never be known. News of Shisun's killing ring provoked dismay in Hunan province. The type of murder conspiracy seen in those provinces was so common that it has its own nickname: Mangjingshi Fanzui.

The other reason for her departure was that she wanted advanced spirited victims, visitors were nice, but too easily. Another reason to leave was that the Chinese government was imposing more restrictions against Tibetans and many of them, in protest were setting themselves ablaze or self-immolation.[22] Zha would not want to be tested about her thoughts of self-immolation, so it was time to leave.

Her Packed Backpack

Zha was ready at age 14, a stolen backpack was loaded with stolen clothes, and her pocket book contained stolen identification and money. Her stolen computer and cell phone (neither which she knew how to operate efficiently but she'd learn), and her bus ticket which was accepted the minute she entered the bus that would eventually arrive in Hong Cong three days, 4 transfers, and a 1,000 miles later. She trilled when the bus driver referred to her as a "student." She looked like the other students in route to Hong Cong.

A young UK boy also traveling to Hong Kong sat next to her on the bus. He explained that he was a computer science major at Wentworth Institute of Technology in Boston but was an exchange student at the City University of Hong Kong. His Mandarin was understandable since in lived in China for two semesters, and he would live in Hong Kong until the semester was over. Then he would return to Boston to finish his last semester before graduation with a masters in computer networking.

He asked her about her computer now on her lap. She explained that she forgot her passwords, "No problem," said he. Each time the bus stopped at rest stops such as Starbucks and during bus transfers, he cleared her computer of viruses, installed antivirus protection agents, and showed her amazing ways to use her computer's networks including cyberspeace activities. The couple spent two nights together during layovers discussing her computer and her cell. She was under the impression that he was a treasure of a boy, but she would learn sometime later that his preference for intimacy was other boys. Her mind was often clouded by an astonishing perseverance to kill him, but too many people knew they were together. He had a lot to teach her which she felt would enhance her search of prey, a word she never used. Her mind never stopped, even as she slept which was only a few hours every night alone.

Hong Kong

Once in Hong Kong, he invited her to stay at his temporary university dorm room at the City University of Hong Kong. They spend a few weeks together – she was learning more about cyberspace, he was busy attempting to see if he were really gay, which he was! She convinced him that she failed him and was truly sorry. She suggested that he should just be accepting that his only lover partners were boys, but she saw in him an "Einstein brilliance," she said. And for his time to help her, she was eternally grateful, but those were not words she necessarily understood.

In the meantime, while he was in class, she toured the campus, kept mental notes about who and where, and actually sat in a few classes. She often comprehended the theme of the instructor's lectures, asked intelligent questions far above her educational experiences which in fact there wasn't any.

Roadways toward a Switch

There were many female students, in particular, from the universities she evaluated, and proceeded to cyberstalk those students and cyberhack their university's records. She skillfully followed her prey. She had a plan in mind that involved a ready to graduate medical student with a high grade point average, a student who was a loner for most part including studying at the library – alone; someone of Chinese heritage but not from Hong Kong because Zha was not up on their urban affairs or its slang, and a student who rarely went home and received no mail. Also, her preferred prey had to have no family or friend visitors including boyfriends. Her cyberhacking after several months proved encouraging when all areas of her interests pointed to Mei-hui Cheng who was about to graduate from The Hong Kong College of Orthopaedic Surgeons and was slated to a surgical internship at Li Ka Shing Faculty of Medicine of the of the University of Hong Kong, in a short time later.

The Switch

Zha emailed the school using Cheng email address requesting that they mail her credentials to her college address. A week later just before graduation, she emailed Cheng using one of her instructor's email addresses that read something like this: we have to talk about something very confidential and personal. Can't do it in my office. Meet me at the main walkway at Ocean Park Road Community Garden (within walking distance from the university) tonight.

At the park, Zha started a conversation with Mei-hui Cheng about the stars, the park, and the weather because it was about to rain. Zha also said she had to particularly give away her vehicle parked on the street because she wasn't a good driver.

Cheng said she was waiting for someone and didn't know when he would arrive, "All he said was tonight. And it looks like it's going to rain." Zha sensed something odd about Cheng, but couldn't put her finger on it. Zha commented that she had an umbrella in her vehicle, and it was parked at the corner. As the two of them strolled to Zha's (stolen) vehicle, Cheng said that she had to keep an eye out for her appointment. It started to rain and Zha suggested they jump in for a second to get out of the rain. Once inside, it was all over for Cheng. In fact, Zha wasn't sure how she was going to get Cheng alone, but the rain worked. She had a plan B, too and certainly a C, D, and F plan too.

Reporting to Work as a Surgical Intern

Dr. Mei-hui Cheng reported to work as a surgical intern at Li Ka Shing Faculty of Medicine of the University of Hong Kong, two weeks later. Zha not only stole Cheng's identity, executed her, and took her new surgeon intern's position at Li Ka Shing Faculty of Medicine of the University of Hong Kong which is a highly rated institution for physicians and surgeons. Cheng's specialty was Orthopedic Surgery. Zha had no medical qualifications, yet moved right into a highly paid internship because of the demand for Chinese nationals and her intellectual ability to adapt.[23] In fact, Zha could have made the perfect U.S. Marine who are trained to improvise, adapt and overcome any obstacle in whatever situation they are needed.

What is an Orthopedic Surgeon?

Probably to respect the successful engagement Zha had with medicine, a brief description of an orthopedic surgeon might prove helpful. An orthopedic surgeon is generally a medical doctor who has continued his or her education and training in a specialized area devoted to the prevention, diagnosis, and treatment of disorders of the bones, joints, ligaments, tendons and muscles. Specifically, "orthopedic surgery is a treatment procedure performed on the musculoskeletal system in case of injuries or carious conditions."[24] The musculoskeletal system includes the bones, the joints, and the following adjacent soft tissues: muscles (which protect and allow movement of bones and joints), ligaments (which connect the bones) and tendons (which connect the muscles to bones). Okay, boy I'm glad that's over, because just learning about the generalities of orthopedic surgeons is mind bogging in itself. Gokarmo Zha better known as Dr. Mei-hui Cheng specialized in knee and hip surgery and as an internist.

Life in Hong Kong

By all accounts, Zha, or should it be said – Dr. Cheng, seemed to enjoy her second profession – surgery, but she became bored with the mundane daily practices of a surgeon. Most knees and hips looked alike and her head was spinning because she really wanted to kill her patients, not cure them. Imagine her frustration and will power! She met and married an almost family physician who moved into her apartment near the hospital. He had long hours because of his internship. Dr. Cheng's schedule as a surgeon started at seven in the morning until 1:00, Monday through Thursday.

This gave her time to hunt for prey at Tsim Sha Tsui which is a shopping and nightlife district in Kowloon, not far from Hong Kong. Some staff members of the hospital frequent that area, therefore, it was not the best location to pursue her goals. She tried Hong Kong Island, but with only two bridges from the mainland to the island, she could be easily apprehended. She also tried hunting in several different directions from Hong Kong, but those areas did not offer her an opportunity to evaluate and stalk her prey. This all made her seem unworthy and unfilled since her whispers from her confined spirits grew louder and louder but failure and apprehension could axe her ambitions.

Dr. Cheng decided to hunt in Tsuen Wan, China  across the Rambler Channel (View taken from Tsing Yi Island and about 20 minutes from Hong Kong). She took an apartment using the stolen credentials of a student named Biyu Liu, but the area was not as lucrative as her home village for prey. But it would do for the time being. She was never paranoid about apprehension but why go out of your way. Because she was bored, she accepted a local detective's offer to smuggle medicine although nothing could ever replace the kill.

Smuggling Medicine

At her Tsuen Wan apartment one afternoon, a local police detective approached Liu (Cheng who was really Zha) as she entered her building. After flashing her badge, she said wanted to talk to Liu in her apartment about an arrangement. Once inside, she laid it out – you were seen leaving a student's apartment at Tsuen Wan Public Ho Chuen Yiu Memorial College. It took the detective some time to track Liu down, "but here I am," and she could be vulnerable was Liu's impression of the detective. The detective clarified that she knew that Liu had no source of income.

According to the detective, major criminal cartels and big time criminals neglect Tsuen Wan. But apparently, the coronavirus pandemic has spiked prices in all aspects of medicine.[25] Her suggestion was that if Liu would help the detective in transporting boxes of cancer medicine to the five hospitals in Hong Kong, she would earn a huge amount of HKD, or yen, or Austrian dollars. Liu said she would do it, but wanted to meet the supplier. The detective said she would check and get back to her. A week later, Liu's smiling face was greeted by the supplier who apparently thought she was a "Niánqīng piàoliang de gūniáng" (pretty young girl). A week later, the supplier was surprised to see Liu without the detective and with her own arrangement. The supplier agreed and the next day, the detective was killed apparently in the line of duty or better yet, in line with Zha's ambition. The old medicine suppliers were eventually replaced with Zha's appointee and that old guard seemed to disappear.

Some of Liu's agents were apprehended as her gang widened but she was never connected to any of them. For instance, a Chinese man had been arrested by customs officials at the Delhi airport for trying to smuggle out anti-cancer medicine worth Rs 1.23 crore.[26] Officials believed he was under the employ of Americans and never considered that he was actually a decoy for a much larger supply of anti-cancer medicine. He didn't know he was a decoy either.

Moved to America

The hospital administrator at Forest Surgery Center in San Jose, California invited Dr. Cheng to consider the chief surgeon's role at the hospital. They visited her twice and she visited the hospital and the area, too. They checked with the Educational Commission on

Foreign Medical Graduates and the hospital and were pleased with what they found. They offered a salary which was enormous, and they agreed to pay her expenses from China to San Jose and her living expenses, too, for serval months. One of her conditions was anonymity, no matter what, above the income. Her new husband went to work in private practice for an old medical school colleague in Sana Clara about a 15 minute drive from their castle like home in the Almaden Valley in San Jose. Dr. Cheng had a hospital vehicle pick her up from her home and return her later in the day.

Her medicine smuggling business was on the high side as was her secret ambition of murder although the number of victims was less than in her homeland, yet neither venture was ever discovered.

Cheng had been employed at Sinai Medical Hospital for almost 10 years before it was discovered, my accident, that she was not a certified surgeon let along a medical doctor at all. The way this arose was an older surgeon, Mildred Henderson, who was the editor of the The BMJ, the leading general medical journal was observing Cheng's unique method of knee surgery. She was going to research Cheng's and five other surgeons' technique for the journal.

Before entering the operating room, Henderson turned to Cheng and complimented her on her amazing career. The ladies spoke a little but before entering the operating room, Henderson commented on Cheng's university thesis for a specialized class. Cheng was not entirely sure what Henderson was referring to and let it pass. "Tell me," asked Henderson, "where did you get the idea from about knee failure? Was it really a bone failure?"

"Yes, yes," Cheng replied. "Everybody knows that."

A few weeks later, Cheng was called into the hospital administers office. There stood Henderson. "Sit down, Dr. Cheng or whoever you are. We have reason to believe that you are in fact not Dr. Cheng. Your response to Dr. Henderson about knee failure had to do with a failure in the bone which was not the thesis argument you made some 15 years ago. Nor is that a response by any real surgeon. We checked your credentials and they were all in order. But one thing stunk out. We know you are female based on the physical exams we are forced to give our surgeons. The Hong Kong College of Orthopaedic Surgeons confirmed that Cheng was a student there but Mei-hui Cheng was actually male and did not have a gender change. Do you want to explain your gender change to us?

Everyone was shocked at the news thinking there was some kind of error or prank being played on the good surgeon. Currently, she awaits sentencing by a local court after a 6 month trial that was highly publicized and on the lips of many professionals and community members. She was found guilty of practicing as a medical specialist when she was not qualified to do so – fraud, and criminally indicted and prosecuted for negligence. She was sentenced to 8 years in prison, and currently is incarcerated at California Institution for Women in Corona, California. She met with an accident of sorts while learning to operate farm equipment in order to work on the prison farm. Apparently, another female prisoner who had never recovered from her failed knee surgery as her leg's range of motion was now particularly gone, and she walked with a cane. The surgeon who performed that operation was Dr. Cheng who lost her leg and left hand in the farm equipment.

COVID-19 Pandemic

It is sad that during the COVID-19 pandemic that many individuals posed as medical doctors, when they have no such background or training. For instance, in one case in Florida, a man who donned a white coat in advertisements that proclaimed he could cure diseases and implied that viruses were of little challenge to him.[27] He declared he could "treat hernias, diabetes, Parkinson's disease, cancer, multiple sclerosis, arthrosis, renal failure, vision problems, and a host of other health issues." Even some real doctors engage in criminal activities. For instance, 6 US doctors were charged in $464m opioid and fake treatment scheme.[28]

Update of Gokarmo Zhaxi

A federal jury found Gokarmo Zhaxi guilty as a fake surgeon who operated 190 times at the Forest Surgery Center in San Jose, California over the past few years.[29] Zhaxi wrote herself glowing references from doctors who existed only in her imagination. Medical authorities at the City University of Hong Kong and

Forest Surgery Center never questioned her "training" from Li Ka Shing Faculty of Medicine of the of the University of Hong Kong.

The court reported that Zhaxi became "obsessed" with the idea of becoming a surgeon but had no time or patience to learn about the discipline. She downloaded forms from the internet and told medical authorities that he had qualified at Li Ka Shing Faculty of Medicine of the University of Hong Kong.

At her trial, Warner Hohen, director of the hospital, said Zhaxi was "diseased" and "a high-grade pathological liar with enormous criminal energies." And he warned: "Hundreds of people have done this in the past and probably will continue to do so."

Zhaxi received a 10 year prison sentence with parole possibilities at the end of the third year of incarceration and fined $1,000,000.

Chapter 4 Adeela Karza and Jalalabad Prison Afghanistan

Overview and War in Afghanistan

Aside from Adeela Karza's generic and demonic spiritual makeup which encouraged her to react to the brutal environment of Afghanistan, the ravages of war might prove helpful in a better understanding of the Taliban girl known as Karza and the children of Afghanistan. Many of those children were born and survived Jalalabad Prison to become suicide bombers and brutal Taliban fighters feared by their enemies more than the seasoned and trained Taliban fighters. A reader might conclude from Chapter 8 that similar circumstances exist for the populations in Guatemala among many other nations on this planet.

At this point in this book many readers might assume that females played a secondary role if any when their nation was engaged in warfare. However, even among the ancient Vikings, archeologists[1] report that

---

[1] The 10th-century Viking's grave contains high quality weapons, an imported uniform, two horses and even a gaming set. Clearly, the grave contained a warrior of great importance; and for over a century, archaeologists assumed the person was male. But when

some of the most feared warriors were female including Viking commanders.[30] In fact, current military warriors engaged in combat can attest to fierce female fighters on both sides in South East Asia and elsewhere.

Nonetheless, Kabul, Afghanistan is classified as one of the most dangerous cities in the world and remains an active war zone along with the surrounding countries such as Syria and Iraq. Afghanistan leaders the Democratic Republic of Afghanistan (DRA) or the Islamic Republic of Afghanistan (IRA) depending on the source of data, label Taliban and ISIS as terrorist organizations that will deliver violence at any moment.[31] DRA or IRA's official languages is Persian or Fārsī. The Taliban rebellion began after they fell from power in DRA following the 2001 war in Afghanistan.

Taliban warriors consisting of men, women, and children are fighting against the Afghan government, led by President Ashraf Ghani, and against the US-led International Security Assistance Force (ISAF). The conflict has spread to neighboring Pakistan and other surrounding countries. The Taliban conduct low-intensity

---

researchers announced in 2017 that the warrior was actually female

warfare against Afghan National Security Forces and their NATO allies. Regional countries, particularly Pakistan, Iran, China and Russia, are often accused of funding and supporting the insurgent groups. The number of horrifying actions by the Afghan military and the Taliban are too numerous to mention but include ruthless attacks on men, women, and children on the streets, in the hospitals, and on the roadways as they migrate away from the danger zones or so they thought.

The Afghan government resumed fighting after a cease fire violation by the Taliban after their horrifying attack by gunmen on a maternity ward run by Doctors Without Borders in Kabul.[32] Mothers and nurses were the main victims in the first attack, with 16 killed. Two of the dead were newborns.

Reasons for Adeela Karza's Safety

Since birth, 12 year old Adeela Karza spent her life in prison similar to many other children. She got the flue, measles and the mumps at Jalalabad Prison in Afghanistan.[33] Adeela Karza's safety at Jalalabad Prison was certain for two reasons. Her mother was Shirin Gul (that's Adeela Karza next to her mother in the image below), a convicted serial killer serving a life sentence, and under Afghan prison policy she can keep her daughter with her until she turns 18.[34]

Gul and her partner Rahmatullah were Karza's parents, although they never married. Both of them were convicted along with her son, her brother-in-law, an uncle and a nephew for their role in the murders and robberies of 27 Afghan men in 2001 to 2004. Afghan prosecutors said she was the ringleader. Working as a prostitute, Shirin Gul brought her customers home and served them drugged kebabs, after which her family members robbed, killed and then buried them in the yards of two family homes. This image is an actual photo of Gul and her daughter, Adeela at Jalalabad Prison.

The second reason for Adeela Karza's safety was because of Adeela, herself and the chattering children in her head and her memories not to mention her experiences with her mother. At Jalalabad Prison, the children she grew up with were also the Muslim Taliban children of convicted alleged offenders of the Afghan government. The difference was that Adeela did not accept being treated like a subservient to the boys at the prison playground. The other girls would come down from the steps of the makeshift slide if a boy stood at the bottom of the steps. Not Adeela. At 7 or 8 she went down the slide and confronted a boy cursing her for her behavior. Boys dominated. He yelled almost in a wine, "دهنت کیرم" (My c..k in your mouth). As she approached him she yelled, "شما دهان در سگ گربه" (Dog shit in your mouth), grabbed his penis, and pulled as hard as she could. When he hit the ground, she jumped on his face and said, "دیگه دفعه" (Next time I'll rip it off). After that incidence, and several similar attacks, Adeela was considered not an agent of Shaitaan (Satan), but the devil herself. Needless to say that Muslims believe that the Devil does exist, and to deny his existence is equal to denying the Qur'an (the central religious text of Islam).[35] She couldn't be an angel since angels, Muslims believe, do not have a free will and therefore it is impossible for angels to disobey God. 'Adeela the Hun' that is the name children called her, could never be an angel.

Salat

Other daily activities for the children at Jalalabad Prison included Salat. For Muslims including children, Salat is the obligatory Muslim prayers, performed five times each day.[36] It is the second Pillar of Islam. God ordered Muslims to pray at five set times of day.[37] During Salat the typical hard core message at the prison and at the madrassas (outside religious schools) which gave birth to the Taliban were the breeding ground for suicide bombers and killers. The message of faith and God is mixed with a hatred of anything outside their own world.[38] The children had a steady diet of anti-western propaganda. They were to fear outsiders and reject anything but the strict teachings of Islam. For the children and probably many adults at Jalalabad Prison, their fear was Adeela the Hun as much as outsiders and Americans and Russians.

Released from Jalalabad Prison

Adeela Karza along with 41 other children were released to the Afghan Child Education and Care

Organization (AFCECO) organization in Kabul which is a respected organization by the government of the Islamic Republic of Afghanistan.[39] None of those children had ever seen a television set, a refrigerator, or tasted an apple. Many young children were transferred to the Parwarishga orphanage, but Adeela Karza lied about her age, her name, and her family and was sent to the orphanage. None of the children in the line with Karza, challenged her perceived lies including the boys. Adeela had no idea how to respond to the world outside the walls of Jalalabad Prison. For Adeela, she had a double whammy: one dealing with a new and uncertain social environment and two, the incessant chattering voices in her spirit letting her know she was never alone. It must have been hard to think through everyday issues with so much chatter pushing her feeding of her decadent appetite towards battle, destruction, and murder.

Karza on the Streets of Kabul

On the streets, Karza dressed and acted as a boy, because females in Afghanistan's were both attacked and had few rights compared to males.[40] Adeela Karza's new name was Afia Karza. In fact, a female's name should not be revealed, even on her grave, another tradition that was met with Karza's resentment.[41] She wore a protective mask since the COVID-19 pandemic altered life everywhere including the official decrees to stay home.

Yet, what added to those chattering voices in her head was the extent of enslavement that females had to accept from their slavers, those making the official decrees and slave orders, as she referred to them. When she learned about the 16-year-old girl at the hospital whose husband cut off her nose and ears, bashed out all but six of her teeth with a stone, and poured boiling water on her, there was no turning back for Adeela Kabul - kill the slavers – men and Allah is male, too. She hit the war-ravaged streets with renewed resolve and a strange energy that seemed to take over her thoughts and her actions. The streets and buildings, what was left of them, resembled her childhood home – Jalalabad Prison.

She would join the war against the Americans although she doesn't recall ever meeting any, but they were ugly men who smoked cigars and violated women just like the slavers in her country. For Afia Karza, her street philosophy which she superficially supported along with other young Taliban boys and their elders is that their religious' duty was to resist the foreign occupation of their homeland. Yet, Afia's real truth encouraged by those chattering voices in her head, was that taking the lives of those ugly Americans and other slavers with a wooden stake or her hands provided love from the spirits who called her in Dari or Persian شفابخش و مقدس روح (sacred spirit and healer).

She loved herself and what she had become while at Jalalabad Prison and recognized that she was coming of age during a time of madness. She felt cheated out of love particularly when her new friends invited him to their family meals. She saw the affection of the family members telling Afia that her way to destroy as many as she could for the love of Karza the girl was her destiny, not Allah, a man. She understood that Islam meant to "surrender, submission, commitment and peace." And that Islam was defined as a path to attain complete peace through voluntary submission to the divine will.[42] Karza understood that she had been submitting to man's rule since she was born, and that now in her freedom, "Kill those slavers and anybody in my path to peace." Little

had anyone known of her genuine philosophy other than
her enemies, "آنها همه کشتن برای و باشید ای حرفه ، باشید مودب
باشید آماده" (be polite, be professional, and be prepared to
kill them all).

Taking a Life is a Controlling Factor

Adeela realized while at Jalalabad Prison and
while on the streets of Kabul that the taking of a life is
the primary controlling factor of this world and the world
beyond this world. Both boys and girls backed up for
'Afia the Hun,' her nickname. A few of those girls joined
a witch cult to counter Afia's powers of domination.
They were promised powers that come after the first time
they killed someone.[43] When Afia learned of the watch
cult and the promise to the girls, somehow those girls
were never seen again, thanks to Afia who had little
practice with her alleged enemies.

There was a common understanding among the
teens and their parents of Kabul that messing with Afia,
could mean your destruction, and you might never be
seen again. Afia was Satan himself, but she had loyal
followers among many boys. Maybe they were awed or
afraid of him and better to be on his safe side which

would benefit their survival. This also meant that no one would complain or tell on Afia as one teen tried only to be attacked by three of Afia's boys who brought the beaten boy to Afia, who finished him off. But, from Adeela's standpoint, those boys similar to Allah (because god is male) were the enemy.

Enlisting in the Taliban

Bring her closer to understanding of her slavers, she along with a few of the boys who followed him, enlistment in the Taliban. They underwent a brief training program in Kunar Province, in northeastern Afghanistan, where one of the boy's father had died during the war against the Soviet Union. He sought revenge, and he privately learned by spying on Afia that he didn't have a

 penis. But he wouldn't carry out his revenge nor would he tell anyone of his findings

because Afia caught him spying and killed him that same day during a training exercise. Afia's trainers applauded him and encouraged Afia in his killing spree but against the enemy – the Afghan Government.

They were trained to become ghosts against the Afghan National Army. Move swiftly, kill as many Afghan's as possible and move out of the area, and then silently move back in. Afghan troops were trapped in an infinite loop, losing and struggling to gain back ground while experiencing huge casualties as they attempt to destroy the Taliban ghosts.[44] The most feared ghost became known as 'Afia the Djinn' of just simple the 'fire creature.' The Djinn, Afghan folklore are fire evil spirits that can't be seen, but are everywhere. Little did the enemy or the Taliban release that this Djinn was not a male but a highly motivated female.

Afia the Djinn Deployed to Korengal

Afia the Djinn and her followers were sent to Korengal, a narrow, cedar-forested valley that harbored one of the U.S. Army's remotest outposts.[45] For more than a year, Afia Karza and her boys conducted ambushes, engaged in firefights, and hid from jets and drones. In one encounter, Afia who seemingly never lost her gender identity had to pretend to pee like boys which

94

she never fully accomplished. She never went naked in the waterways when the boys were around and most of the time she washed herself in those waterways with her clothes on. She lost a dozen friends but 42 Americans were killed and hundreds were wounded in the Korengal, which was referred to as the Valley of Death. Eventually, the Americans surrendered it to the Taliban.

At 17, Afia Karza was an accomplished Taliban solider. His (they believed she was a he) bravery was noted by her followers and Taliban soldiers and officers. One maneuver of Afia was to disguise himself as Afghan security officer and he would eliminate several high ranking American officers.[46] Her savage attacks upon the enemy became common knowledge adding to her remarkable warrior skills and adding to the Afia the Djinn legend. It might have been rumored at least among the female Taliban fighters that Afia might have been a female as she was developing breasts and tried to hide her minstrel cycle, but no one would challenge her.

Aiding Wounded Soldiers

Afia Karza often helped bandage her bleeding followers from battle. Many of them referred to her as

بزرگ مبارز یک و پزشک یک روح (the spirit of a doctor and a great warrior). Many would go into battle with her and many would protect her from enemy fire. Little had many of known that she was in all her greatest, when she was engaged in combat. But she also aided those boys who required medical help. A passionate Afia was somewhere inside that warrior they said, but the truth was that aiding the wounded had other benefits such as helping them die!

The allies captured one of those hospital type units where Afia was busy aiding the wounded. As the wounded were being moved from the unit, they called out to Afia, "کنم می تعظیم خود محافظ و پزشک عالی روح به." (I bow to the great spirit of my doctor and protector).

A Russian officer herd the remark and approached Afia. In poor Persian, he asked, "هستید؟ دکتر یک شما شما" (You are a doctor?) A few of the wounded responded before she did because they knew Afia wanted to lunge and take the life of the officer along with a few of his warriors "دکتر بله" (Yes, doctor) they spoke out.

The Russian officer told Afia to follow him to his commander. Once learning his skills as a doctor, she was told again in poor Persian to help the wounded Russian soldiers and they would not kill the 25 wounded Taliban rebels. She agreed and went to work. A few days later, she was sent to the Allies medical station at the Kabul airport where she quickly built her knowledge of mending.

Afia was in Training to be a Spy

The Russians decided that Afia would serve the motherland better as a Russian spy. She was told that she would be diligently trained on a computer and networking so much so that she could hack into Taliban and American networks, and they would teach her to drive. Then Afia provided her conditions: a Syrian passport, a Syrian birth certificate, a medical doctor's certificate from Damascus Hospital in Damascus in Syria, his name entered as Adeela Karza, a female not a male, and her name entered into Damascus Hospital's graduates. At first they resisted, but she wouldn't back down. She entered intelligence school in Moscow and was returned to the Taliban battlefield as Dr. Adeela Karza and as a skillfully trained intelligence officer, a few months later.

Dr. Adeela Karza the Spy and Bounty of American Troops

In the field, she was immediately at work and shared information with her Russian handler on a local network. She advised her handler that Taliban warriors were dressed in American uniforms and would be at such and such location. The Russians quickly reacted and eliminated the American squad in the middle of the night. Had any of them been sophisticated enough to examine their trophies, they would have realized that they were indeed Americans and not Taliban warriors. She, now requested the bounty for the death of American soldiers that Russian military intelligence unit secretly offered to Taliban-linked militants.[47] The Russians were in no position to refuse her request which also encouraged her to provide more data to the various Russian military units and more bounty for Dr. Karza.

In Karza's way of thinking, the Taliban warriors were her people not the Americans. As a cyberpredator, she took full advantage of hacking into Russian, American, and their allies' website and caused as much destruction as possible. For instance, she searched online for and found higher level officers and advised them to meet with lower level officers and spies, and she killed them all. Her cyberpredator skills were as great a weapon as the Russian or Americans rockets or drones. She liked her the surreptitious conduct especially when it ended in the destruction of her enemies.

Damascus Hospital

As things heated up for Dr. Karza, she left the area and walked into the Damascus Hospital in Damascus, which is one of the largest hospitals in Syria. It is linked to the Faculty of Medicine at Damascus University.[48] Both welcomed one of their own to aid in the ER. Dr. Adeela Karza became the chief medical practitioner at the ER. She made it clear to the hospital staff that she would take the final steps in determining the triage of any patient especially military. She also made it clear that all healthcare personnel and security officers in the ER reported to her alone. In this fashion, she would take the lives of some without question. The hospital administration was grateful for her employment, and the good doctor said she wanted no pay. One reason for her generosity probably had to do with appearance as the compassion sort, and the notion that she should have asked the Russians for a social security number. At this time in the doctor's life, she was 20 years old. Heaven's gates were open to her and sitting on heaven's throne was a wicked wizard named Adeela Karza who answered only to the chattering children in her head. The reasons the hospital accepted her without question may have been due to the extreme shortage doctors and medical healthcare practitioners because of the war in Afghanistan.

War and Medicine

War in the Middle East which comes and goes often with different players on both sides, but the casualty rate among noncombatants, children, and students including those in medical school is something a wicked wizard would find meritorious. For instance, the Syrian Civil War, which ended sometime in 2015 but groups continue to battle each other. A United Nation Commission of inquiry reports that all parties to the civil war "committed war crimes - including murder, torture, rape and enforced disappearances. They have also been accused of using civilian suffering - such as blocking access to food, water and health services through sieges - as a method of war."[49] This and other similar backdrops, convinced Dr. Adeela Karza that the premature death of innocent men, women, and children can be glorified in the spirit of the undead.

Some of those actions caused a massive shortage of medical equipment, doctors, medicine and electricity throughout the Middle East. One count reports that nearly 800 medical personnel have been killed.[50] In Syria alone, 30,000 doctors are thought to have left the country since the conflict began. Many medical school students dropped out. In fact, 100 out of 400 students had left the school. This data makes it easy to understand why Dr. Karza was prized by her employer and everyone else for that matter.

Part II: Fake Children

Chapter 5 Morgan Spencer and Abandoned Trailer Parks

Morgan Spencer was adapted at age 10 from Pathfinders in Milwaukee, Wisconsin. Pathfinders is a children's home that rallies around the idea of "There is no wrong door to enter Pathfinders."[51] Morgan's new family, the Weiers lived in Wales, Wisconsin about 30 miles west from Milwaukee, and about 30 miles northwest from Morgan's birth home in Watertown. Matt Weier works for the state as a highway patrol officer, his wife, Marilynn is a school teacher at Kettle Moraine High School, and their 7 year old daughter Anissa Weier, a mildly autistic child is in second grade at Wales Elementary School. Matt and Marilynn discussed it for some time among themselves and with their friends at RiverGlen Christian Church – Anissa needed an older sister mainly because the both of them were away from home for long periods of time. Both Matt and Marylyn taught bible studies at RiverGlen and had for some time. Particularly Marylyn who was born in Wales, and once her and Matt started dating in their first year at Concordia University Wisconsin in Mequon, Wisconsin after 45 miles from Wales, they were inseparable, very much in love, and Matt watched Marylyn as she instructed bible classes. Eventually, he began instructing, too.

In their pursuit of "the right child for Anissa," Marylyn send emails to several of the children's home in Wisconsin. They were not swayed by the three girls they interviewed and sent apologetic emails to their respective

 children's home. They received an email from a private source about Morgan Spencer, a bright 10 year old who had lost her parents in an automobile accident. Her picture was included in the email. The email said that Morgan Spencer could be dropped off at their home the following day at 10:00AM or 4:00PM their choice.

Morgan proved to be the child the Weier's absolutely sought, but they were emailed after she left that another family had a strong interest in Morgan and they were

planning on visiting the children's home in the morning. "Isn't there anyway to speed up our adaption of this amazing child."

The response was, "Yes, complete the attached forms, and use a debt (preferred) or credit card to forward the $580.00 fees to us. As soon as we review your data and the fees are collected, we will notify you as to our decision." First thing in the morning, Morgan rang their door bell wearing a backpack and holding her computer bag. "Oh my gosh, honey," Marylyn screamed in her excitement, "come in, please. We are so happy you're here." Later Marylyn would call the school and her husband who was probably somewhere in Wisconsin about Morgan.

Morgan knew her way to her new bedroom and asked about Anissa. "Oh she's in school, honey, and once you've settled in, I'll take you to school. Most assuredly, you would be able to start 4th grade right away."

"Oh, that would be amazing, Mrs. Weier."

"You hush now, we'll none of that Mrs. Weier stuff. It's Marylyn and once you feel comfortable with me, maybe you might refer to me as 'mom,' but only," her head moved back and forth, "if I earned it."

When Anissa came home from school, it was a wonderful meeting of the two 'sisters.' "Now you know, Morgan, I usually work during the day and you and Anissa, your new sister will be alone till I get here. That would be about 30 or 40 minutes later because the high school is on a different time schedule than the elementary school."

As time passed, Morgan eventually called Marylyn, mom, but she didn't call Matt, dad, at least not yet. She wanted him to beg, and she was really good at manipulating people, even cops. School for Morgan went well, and her teacher reported that Morgan was extremely bright and possessed the mind of a child much older than her actual age. In fact, Morgan was 16 years old not 10, and she was never admitted to any children's home nor were her parents killed in an auto accident.

Morgan's Parents on the Run

Morgan was born in September at an abandoned trailer park at the outskirts of Albuquerque, New Mexico to Michelle and Jesús Pérez who were squatters and on the run from the Mexican authorities for the murder of police officers and rape and murder while on the run. According to the federal police reports, 13 Mexican police officers were killed in an ambush in Michoacan as five police vehicles were traveling through the municipality of Aguililla. They were ambushed by more than 30 armed individuals.[52] Two of those armed individuals were Michelle and Jesús Pérez.

According to reports, Michelle who was obviously pregnant at the time and Jesús Pérez apparently seemed burdened by their 5 years old daughter. When the couple ran into some of the elite members of rebel team, asked about their 5 year old daughter, Victoria. One of the members, proceeded to rape the child in front of her parents, and dismembered her body. Forensic reports later revealed that the pretty little girl had been "dosed with meth, raped, strangled, stabbed and dismembered."[53] Michelle and Jesús Pérez had sex with their child's rapist and slit his throat while he was having a climax. What the Mexican and now American authorities discovered was that Michelle and Jesús Pérez allegedly recruited men to have sex with their daughter via the dating site, 'Plenty of Fish.'

Abandoned Trailer Parks

They lived in various abandoned trailer parks, houses, and offices and churches around the area for five years and eventually landed in South Carolina. Often other Mexican resistance fighters brought them food and medicine while in New Mexico. The rest of the time, they ripped off, bartered, and harmed anyone not cooperating with their survival. You might say that Morgan's early childhood was surrounded by fifth, violence, and ignorance. But there's more, particularly about Morgan. Her parents had great difficulty with her strong personality and intense demands upon them. Morgan often had hour long meltdowns when she would go crazy.[54] Her family learned to ignore her and supplied no supervision or concern for her welfare. Morgan came and went and sometimes for a day or two at in her convince.

Her family never suspected, however that Morgan was the greater monster particularly as they migrated toward the east states such as South Carolina. For example, at 6 she dropped tears and podded lips in front of a 9 year old boy with a piece of cake in his hands, which pushed the boy into vulnerability (as planned) in the woods near one of the Pérez's makeshift homes. She bite his neck so hard and in rapid succession that he couldn't move. Once on the ground, she pushed his eyes into his skull and ate the cake as she sat on his stomach. She apparently hid the body in the swaps since a boy's body was never discovered.

At 7, Morgan left her 1st grade class at Lexington Middle during lunch and recess. She knew where she was headed as planned from earlier observations. This time, at the playground in the forest behind school, Morgan watched a 6 year old girl and her mother. Morgan noticed that her mother was continually engaged in a conversation on her cell. The only child at the playground liked the slide, and once she went down it, she ran around it out of sight. That's when Morgan grabbed her between the legs with one hand and her other hand covered her mouth as she pulled the child into the brush. The more the child wiggled and tried to get away, Morgan moved her now free hand behind the child's head while the other hand stayed firm on her mouth. She twisted her head enough so that her victim stopped wiggling. She filled her mouth with mud, pushed her eyes through her face, and covered her with leaves. Morgan headed back to her school, and made it just in time since lunch time and recess was over.

A few days later, she heard some of the teachers talking about the disappearance of a 6 year child, named Fannie Sedevic, in Lexington, South Carolina.[55] Morgan's insides were doing flips and she felt very happy to know that no one else knew what she knew about the missing child.

Morgan's Bedroom Walls

Wherever Morgan lived with Michelle and Jesús

 Pérez, she wrote and painted on the walls not only where she slept, but all over the living quarters no matter how humble they were. She wrote and painted with pins, paint brushes, and screw drivers.

When younger she largely scribbled and as she aged, she wrote and painted strange and bazaar things that she created in her head. Morgan scribbled thoughts (and misspelled many words) about someone she called slendergirl and how to summon her.[56]

She wrote that it works better at night to summon her. Go into the woods, and carve a circle into a tree and put and X through it. Press your face against the circle with your eyes closed. Then turn around to see slendergirl.

Computer Theft

Along with destroying her home's walls, she learned how to use a computer in 2nd grade and at night, she broke in sliding through a narrow window and took her teacher's computer. She became fixated in the use of it and often had to walk close to school in order to get on signal. When she had questions, she would ask at school. Her cyber space became her new conjuring sight for victims and fun which actually were one in the same for her. She learned how to hack into her school's data base along with other data bases that interested her. One way she accomplished her hacking skills, is that she would tell her teacher that she didn't know what happened while she was on her computer, but suddenly she was in some strange sight that looked like the school. The teacher would run through what she could remember, and aid in getting to that sight. Remember, Morgan is a very amiable child, with smiles to match her manipulative charms.

Morgan and Anissa

Morgan is extremely bright as you already realize, but her dark joys should be enough to convince anybody of her sinister and punishing mission to cleanse the earth of any goodness. For example, she charmed Anissa Weier so much so that Anissa would literally climb hell's gate with Morgan. Morgan taught Anissa about slendergirl and how to bring her to life. When Anissa couldn't see slendergirl, she was told that it was her fault because she didn't believe and she was not to tell her parents about slendergirl. Morgan described a slender, tall, girl without a face but long arms and legs. For those who don't believe, slendergirl will find them in the thick of the night and cut their hair. "You don't want that do you, Anissa?"

Morgan read pieces to Anissa that also summoned creepypastas. Creepypasta was Morgan's way to describe a nightmare story she read on the internet and was found in a child's dream.[57] Both of their favorite stories from Creepypasta was The Seed Eater and White with Red.

Morgan and Anissa the Killers

Privately Morgan explained to Anissa that an attack on the girl was to appease 'slendergirl.' Morgan Spencer and Anissa Weier led their victim to the woods under the pretense of a game of hide and seek.[58] The girls pinned the 8 year old girl down and Morgan stabbed her 10 times, and the wounds were so deep that the handle broke off her knives, leaving the blade embedded in Morgan's victims. "What a trip, right? Now do it as hard as me," she said to Anissa. As Anissa stabbed, Morgan encouraged her to stab harder and deeper. Morgan wanted her to laugh and she did, the entire time while looking at Morgan for her approval and while stabling the girl 19 times in the face. Morgan explained to Anissa that if she ate the eyes of the girl that Anissa would have eternal happiness. "You want to be happy?"

Update

Morgan and Anissa went door to door asking about babysitting jobs. When individuals said that maybe, Morgan turned to Anissa, "Okay, plug their phone into your cell." She entered maybe five numbers and they were happy. When a soldier said he had to check with his wife who wasn't home, Morgan and Anissa accepted his hospitality of a couple of Cokes. He had three girls the oldest is 6 and they could use a babysitter. Little Morgan was curious about men in uniform or maybe just men. Morgan asked about the furniture in the children's room. "It looks really pretty from what I saw of it through the window." The soldier said, "Take a closer look, ladies," as finger pointed toward the room.

"Wait for me," she said to Anissa.

"As soon as the unsuspecting soldier and Morgan entered the bedroom, she wrapped her arms around him and her little body only reached the area around his belly button. She bite him gently, actually thinking that she would bite him to death. Her curiosity was to actually kill this soldier, and his thoughts were apparently centered on something else. He reached to touch her face and she

113

didn't scream even would when his hands slid down her little body. She helped and ripped her own clothes from her body and smacked her own face. Now she screamed and when Anissa heard it, she called 9-1-1. "My girlfriend is being attacked," said she when asked, "What is your emergency."

The cops were there in no time and Anissa opened the door and pointed in the direction of her Morgan and the soldier. Morgan trembled with every word as she that had been attacked. The soldier, Daniel Kemp, 51, of Cameron, North Carolina was arrested and eventually sentenced to life in prison for aggravated sexual assault of a minor. [59]

.

Chapter 6 Absinthe the Child Killer in Manhattan

Overview and Her Fake Struggle: Serving God

Absinthe, a 7th grader living in Manhattan, one of the five boroughs at New York City, read Moraine Stephenson, a journalist's account of 15 year old Alyssa Bustamante who dug a grave and waited for a victim.[60] Absinthe was fascinated with Bustamante despite her never really knowing her, but she understood her – one predator to another. Stephenson at the New York Times went on to write that Bustamante was pretty and very bright, but Bustamante had a "dangerous psychosis" and fantasized about killing someone, anyone. Funny, the 12 year old Absinthe thought, "That's what I wanna do. And I wanna smell their breath when they're losing it."

When Absinthe continued reading Stephenson's account of Bustamante's psychological profile, Absinthe literally screamed and cut herself with a pen on her forearm in the school's computer room. "WTF," she said slowly not wanting to attract attention. "All these fake creeps know so much about everyone without ever even, like, meeting them." Absinthe decided it was showtime – time to kill Moraine Stephenson for her crime against Bustamante and all the other girls who wanna dig a grave and wait for a victim. Absinthe's motivation to kill was allegedly cored in her assessment of others who wanted to define them and were lam in their idea. When she might come to that conclusion about anyone, killing them would stop the lies. In reality, wickedness among evil spirits never die,

Absinthe thought to herself about her enemies who named her 'Absinthe' with a huge hate feelings for her mother and her mother's girlfriend - Gwynn. At 12, she learned that real alcohol made from Absinthe is not illegal, but it can't be sold in bars and liquor stores.[61] Some called it the devil in a little green bottle. She felt that she heard her enemies mention that thought more than once. She was the devil in a little green dress! She never realized it at the time, but today, she likes what she hears. She also learned that a French newspaper, reported that Absinthe, is "The premiere cause of bloodthirsty crime in this century."[62] "So I will live up to the name – a wicked demon who takes no prisoners," whispered Absinthe to herself.

A School Assignment

Rather than working on assignment on the computer at school, she cyberhacked into Stephenson's websites for information. Her fingers slid over the keys with ease, and when the teacher began to walk towards her, she quickly pressed alt+tab and her screen switched back to the assignment page. When Absinthe finally came across Stephenson's photo at LinkedIn, she whispered to the photo, "182 (I hate you) bitch, and you're going to meet the wicked demon, Absinthe, and I'm going to love every one of the 127 seconds to your death for what you said about Alyssa."

Absinthe found Stephenson's photo at Truthfinder, Facebook, and CheckPeople. She worked fast and hard and eventually also found Stephenson's location and her home address after hacking into the book publisher. But that wasn't really necessary since Stephenson published through Amazon.com as an independent author, Absinthe learned – she was an open book!

The more she learned about Stephenson, the more she wanted to taste her disgusting blood and watch with joy, Stephenson's eyes fade to blank. "What'a serial chiller! I'm buzzen!" She felt that when Stephenson's blood finally would touch her lips, her insides would turn to white.

At home, still pushing grave thoughts through her head about Stephenson, Absinthe glared at herself in the mirror, and caught her eyes widen as a tear meandered down her pretty cheek. She remembered the last time a tear streamed down her check. That was when she decided to strangle that ugly little first grader, Billy Winters. That time, her defense to her teacher was that he was trying to play with her private parts, and "I just didn't know what to do," her sad little lips whispered out. She had to find a new excuse if caught after killing Stephenson. She decided to search the web for what other children had said, and alter their lame excuses to fit her murder of that lame duck of a writer. Her little fingers brushed over her computer keys like fire on rain. She stopped. She found it: "My mother beat me all the time and this Stephenson lady seemed like my mother when

118

she raised her hands. I had to push hard to get away from her."

Absinthe's Early Childhood Experiences

Absinthe was born to a 17 year old single girl named Nanine in the back sit of a car parked in an ally, while her mother was busy satisfying some wacko customer. Once home, her mother left her on the floor and had to shoe-away, Tiny, their little dog. It was a small two bedroom apartment on the third floor of an apartment house in Manhattan. Nanine's mother who was confined to a wheelchair and a feeding tube because of her leukemia and muscular dystrophy lived with her. Also, Nanine's love partner, Gwynn, and Gwynn's two sons were residents as well. It was never quiet and continual ramblings filled the air at virtually all hours of the day and night. Whoever bought groceries home had to guard them, which meant that the younger children such as Absinthe and Gwynn's sons Jeff and Jesse, were at the mercy of Nanine and Gwynn assuming they were somewhat awake. Gwynn attempted to give her sons poison as sweets, but Nanine's mother was making a load commotion from her wheelchair. Gwynn stopped.

Same thing with privacy – there wasn't easy and that included Nanine and Gwynn's intimate moments. They tried to keep their most serious moments hidden from the others but only if the bathroom was empty, yet the locks never worked.

At 3 Years of Age

At 3 years of age, Absinthe learned that she was different from others including the little girls her mom and Gwynn brought home for whatever reason. Maybe babysitting jobs. She attacked Jeff, one of Gwynn's sons with her hands to his little throat. The other son, Jesse, hid in the closest. Absinthe wouldn't let go of Jeff when Gwynn tried to separate them. Absinthe felt like a real person for the first time in her little life. She learned that she was someone feared by Gwynn's boys and Nanine and Gwynn's visiting little girls, who all kept their distance, but in a tiny apartment, Absinthe could harass and attack at will.

She told Nanine's mother that she wanted to bite those little kids, "Hard. I wanna taste their raw blood," and her tongue wiped her lips with a snickered. But the most fun was when Absinthe said those words, and repeated the phase many times over the years, she always felt an icy chill slip and slid down the center of her back to the center of her legs. When that happened, she locked her thighs together and wanted for the chill to scatter. Sometimes she said to herself, "No, noni, don't go away." Sometimes, she would repeat those words more than once when alone.

Sometimes, Absinthe would push Nanine's mother's wheelchair into the bathroom and tell her that she was going to drown her in the toilet bowl. Then Absinthe became very excited with her actions, and pricked each of her toes below the nails and laughed some more as Nanine's mother wormed in her wheelchair witnessing dabs of blood sprouting from Absinthe's little toes.

Nanine said that Absinthe was "just going through a phase. She didn't mean it." And she told Gwynn that Absinthe would never hurt her boys.

At 4 Years of Age

At 4, during daycare recess at school, a garden snake appeared in the grass and all the children ran except Absinthe. She grabbed it, ran after the other children, and once she caught up with a slow girl, she wanted, no demanded that the girl bite its head off. Teachers ran to the girl's aid and tried to calm her down while all the time Absinthe was laughing and saying things like, "Scaredy cat, scaredy cat, your mother wears diapers…. Baby!"

At home Absinthe had enough of the "Stupid dog, Tiny." While Nanine and Gwynn were in the bathroom together, she scratched the face of the dog with a folk and then plugged the folk into the dog's eye. She twisted his neck and through it out the window. Days later when Gwynn asked about Tiny, Absinthe said he ran out of the apartment and she couldn't catch him. Gwynn went, "Oh, okay," and gently shrugged her shoulders.

Accused of Strangulation

By the time she was five, she was accused of struggling to death one of Gwynn's sons. Absinthe blamed her mother, Nanine, for the killing. Said Nanine was in a "fit of craziness and that's when it happened." Of course, Absinthe waited until Nanine and Gwynn to black-out from their drugs and their bad sex and that's when Absinthe killed Gwynn's son, Jeff who was in the

122

bathroom. Absinthe was not horrified when choking Jeff, but she lost control of bodily functions. She cupped it up in her hands and pushed it down his throat.

Prosecutors learned that Nanine and Gwynn worked the streets for an income and were high on cocaine most of the time. Department of Social Services stepped in and removed Nanine's wheel chaired mother and removed her feeding tubes, "She doesn't need these things," one of the DSS workers said matter-of-factly. Absinthe assumed that a miracle had happened because Nanine's mother was cured without ever thinking that her mother, Nanine, forced the old woman into the chair as a method gaining her disability income.

Absinthe and Jesse Placed in a Children's Home

The DSS workers took Jesse and Absinthe to a children's home and eventually placed them in a single family home together. No one wanted to split Jesse and Absinthe up thinking they were brother and sister. In their new home, Absinthe ruled and Jesse knew better than to make up his own mind about anything recalling what happened to his brother. Their new guardians and Absinthe and Jesse's counselor thought it was fantastic that the boy listened to Absinthe, but those guardians nor the counselor ever realized that Jesse was under a real life treat to comply with his 'sister.' Sometimes, Absinthe would enter the bedroom of her 'brother' and play 'strangulation' with him. Who would tell on Absinthe? "Say it," as his head was locked between her pajamaed thighs, "Say it. My sister is awesome." Once he said it, Absinthe jumped from his bed and jumped into her own bed.

School

Jesse and Absinthe attended the same elementary school, but different grades. Jesse, a quiet shy boy always supported Absinthe when she didn't attend class and when other school kids complained about her abusiveness. Jesse learned his lines well, "Absinthe was 'bummed' because of our family life. She was no splatterpunk, so don't say anything bad about her." From Absinthe's perspective, she couldn't care less how Jesse supported her emotionally or otherwise. Jesse realized that he and their new family members quickly learned that they lived with a dragon that could breathe fire down their throats particularly when they slept. Some of 'their' family members worked out a routine, one slept while another stayed awake to guard against the dragon. They were trying to get out of their commitment to DSS about Absinthe, but it was kind of counterproductive because DSS was under the impression that Absinthe was a sweetheart and many families wanted to adapt her and Jesse. How could they bring evidence forward that sweet Absinthe rivaled the 'mouth' of hell? And how much money would they lose by attempting to end their contract with DSS? During the family's interviews with Absinthe which also included a social worker's interview, there were no signs what-so-ever emanating from Absinthe's words or behavior that could be linked to violence, unhappiness, or blaming others about her circumstances. If only those interviewers understood predatoral intent and their manipulation expertise regardless of age!

Third Grade

In reality, Absinthe loved who she was and the way she lived because she did whatever she wanted including playing strangulation with others whom she called the 'toilet babies.' The toilet babies included the kids on the playground who needed attention – yes, she was able to determine vulnerability similar to many predators. Teachers, counselors, and other providers had no clue about the hold Absinthe held over her schoolmates, and for that matter the controls she had over her family members including Jesse, Nanine, and Gwynn.

She often went out of her way to terrorize kids including one teacher whom Absinthe felt was a milksop (weakling) and she was right. The teacher left her post after Absinthe's attack. Also, while in third grade, Absinthe, the killer Absinthe, during recess popped from behind the swings and grabbed a third grader by the throat for cutting inline. The teachers were shocked about her strength and her perseverance toward cruelty as she held on to the throat of her victim even as the teachers were pulling her off the child. They were shocked, too, by Absinthe's vocabulary, because Absinthe always presented a picture of a very sweet and a compassionate child, and now it was as if she were possessed by a demon of sorts. The school counselor waited to see

126

Absinthe's guardians to discuss the matter. During the meeting, Absinthe was a perfect angel and explained that her victim said he was going to drop a bomb in class. Absinthe never saw the boy again in class. He was probably dismissed from school based on sweet Absinthe's performance and several other students supporting Absinthe's comment about the boy. They too learned their lines well, as excepted – "Yes, he said he was going to bomb the school."

Absinthe Mastered Her Craft

It took Absinthe many attempts to actually kill another child through strangulation. Sometimes when she left a victim, she didn't really know if her victim was dead or alive. She learned that external signs of strangulation are generally absent in over half of all victims, she read on line, "even when examined by skilled medical personnel alerted to the possibility of strangulation injury."[63] She learned that she had to hold on to the jugular vein for 7–14 seconds from strangulation to have the victim pass out, and in the following 2 minutes or so for them to die.[64] Thank goodness for the internet, she thought to herself. Once

Absinthe learned about the time factor, she always smiled to herself that she's down for the count. And yes, she counted and would not attack a victim unless she knew that she had a least 127 seconds with her prey. Some of her prey simply died from their own panic not knowing actually what was or what happened to them while others were so scared that they never told a soul.

5th and 6th Grades

The school administrators where Absinthe was about to enter 5th grades realized that they had two dilemmas: Absinthe's behavior and her new family who donated large sums of money to the school district and the political juice of New York City including the mayor himself. In private, some administrators, Absinthe's teacher, and PE coach discussed what their options. At the end of the meeting, it was concluded that they only had to deal with her for two years and then she'd be off to middle school. They made a pack that they would be in conversation with each other as Absinthe events would unfold. They individually hoped that Absinthe would behave in some way that could be considered criminal and then their troubles might be over. "But we must give this poor dear an opportunity to complete the school year without an incident. Keep a tight monitor on her." They all agreed, and a "Right, right, right," was heard as they left the meeting room.

Things went well till the third week at school in the girl's bathroom. One girl slapped Absinthe for an incidence in 2nd grade. Two girls supporting the slapper jumped in and slapped Absinthe, too. Absinthe literally jumped on the biggest of the girls and spit on the other two who then they ran out of the bathroom leaving their friend. When a teacher arrived, Absinthe said, "Go ahead and tell her what you did." The tearful girl remained silent for a moment. "Fine, do you want me to tell her what you did?" The girl was probably deciding who she wanted to be disciplined by – Absinthe or the teacher. Absinthe won.

She nodded at Absinthe suggesting she wanted her to tell the teacher what happened.

"K," said Absinthe, "she slid under one of the toilet doors and pushed the girl off the stool."

The teacher turned to the girl and asked, "Is that true?"

She looked at Absinthe before answering, "Yes ma'am."

Absinthe never saw the girl again at school, and when she saw her two friends they did everything possible to avoid Absinthe.

Summer Time at Central Park

During the summer months between 6th and 7th grade, Absinthe spent time at Central Park, one of her favorite places for the hunt particularly when it rained. She loved the rain but in many ways it camouflaged her attacks she learned that other predators, although she didn't know that term, were also in the park, and they avoided each other. They liked the rain, too. It should come as no surprise that Absinthe had no friends who wanted to spend time with her probably because they feared for their lives.

Since Absinthe lived in Manhattan right near 79th Street and Central Park Avenue one of the main entrances for the park, she would wander through the park, alone. She always marveled at the Belvedere Castle close to where she would enter. She loved the Alice in Wonderland bronze sculptures, and the Central Park Zoo. But those were not good places to hunt because there was nowhere to hide, and there were too many parents.

Her attacks were usually short and the restrooms which had more than one entrance so she was able to mix in with the kids on either side of all the 20 restrooms located in the park. Her favorite restroom was at the Loeb Boathouse because children were allowed to run crazy all around the boathouse sometimes while caretakers were in boats. She became a vigilant observer and psychological evaluator in search of vulnerable prey. Only once during summer session between 6th and 7th grade was she able to attack a girl has she opened the door to leave the toilet stall. There was no one around at the time, so that was perfect. You see, Absinthe learned to master her trade with ease. Calmly, she left the stall, washed her hands, and exited slowly. Another time in another restroom, she pulled a girl about her size by the angles through the toilet door and jumped on her. In moments, as the adrenaline rush crashed all over her body, her hands were already around the throat of the child, and she buried them deep under the girl's cheeks. Once leaving the restroom as some others came in, one ran after Absinthe and asked, "Did you see any strange person in the bathroom? Something happened in there."

"Yea," said she in her little girl's voice "It was a black guy. He almost knocked me over."

The Murder of Moraine Stephenson the New York Times Street Journalist

Absinthe knew that physically she was no match for Stephenson. So her death had to come as both a surprise and it had to be certain death – the full count of 127 seconds plus 20 more just to be sure. Absinthe had two advantages: Stephenson didn't know her, and Absinthe wanted to kill her. She considered a knife but if she didn't stick Stephenson just right, she could fight back. She needed help. She decided to return to her computer and plugged in Children who kill. The site she chose was "Children who kill - From shootings to stranglings, 12 evil kids and how they took another young life."[65]

Following are some of the things Absinthe read and commented about: Joshua Phillips was 14 when he murdered an eight year old and hid her body for six days, it was doubtful that she could hid Stephenson's body. Jon Venables and Robert Thompson were 10 when they killed two-year-old James Bulger and Morgan. No way could Absinthe compare a 2 year old's death to Stephenson, she was 38 years old and looked fit.

Finally, after searching the web, with a number of posted phases, such as can you kill someone with a robe? She found this:

"You mean garrote wires? Of course you can. It's the same principle as with a rope. Wrap around neck and pull tight until the person stops breathing. Wire can be damn strong and it's damn near impossible to dig loose from you neck if held tight." [66]

Then Absinthe had to decide - the where. Absinthe learned after cyberstalking Stephenson more that she drove her car every Sunday at 10:00 in the morning, to visit her ailing mother who lived in Rego Park in Queens, about a 10 mile drive. After more web searches and considerable acting out of the murder of

Stephenson, she decided to attack Stephenson in her condo's outside garage facility. Absinthe could easily find Stephenson's red BMW i8 Coupe convertible. At Google maps linked to Stephenson's address, she clicked 'streetview' to get a picture of the lay of the land and the parking lot which is behind the Olmstead Condominiums at 382 Central Park West. "So this dead person must make a lot of money and have an amazing view of my city," whispered Absinthe to herself.

The moment of truth for Stephenson finally arrived. Absinthe was prepared with a garrote wire tucked in to her belly. She dressed like a boy and wore sport outdoor sandals. Under her jeans she wore tight workout paints. She could drop her jeans with ease. She cut her hair so it could all tuck in her hat. She wore a Yankee baseball hat covering her eyes and much of her face.

She boarded the subway at 86th street near her home and existed it at 96th street near Stephenson's home. As she approached Stephenson's car at the exact time she would be leaving for her mother's, she waved at her, and as planned fell to the cement and screamed. On the cement, she retrieved her killing wire and rubbed a reddish color paint resembling blood on her face. As expected, because Absinthe knew Stephenson was a 'caring person,' she approached the boy on the ground. "Oh my," feverishly said she. Stephenson crouched down over Absinthe's face. At that moment, Absinthe quickly put her wire around her victim's neck and pulled hard. The idea was to get Stephenson's face to hit the cement and maybe unconscious. Absinthe was already counting. It was after her 127 seconds someone approached the two of them. "What's up?" a person asked.

"My auntie, fell and hit her head. Can you help me?" Absinthe revealed a thought she had prepared in advance just for this moment.

As the stranger who now appeared to be a garage attendant helped Stephenson up, he realized that she was completely unresponsive and the young man disliked the blood on his white shirt. Absinthe stood and walked away saying, "I'm going to fetch my uncle, he can help. Hang on to her, dude." Making the curve of the parking to enter the street, from the jean pocket she removed a blond wig and dropped the jeans and the hat as planned. She was no longer a boy, but a happy very happy young blond 'thing' with cute tanned, long legs. She skipped all the way to the subway. She was amazed as to how she felt while Stephenson was dying. When she took in her breath, she felt a sensation in her body reaching down to her legs. She thought, "This must be what sex is about but this way, I'm the boss of my feelings not some stupid boy or whatever."

Chapter 7 Devanna Volkov the Russian Child Predator

Overview

Devanna Volkov's life began when she was abducted as a baby from her stroller at Tts Beyker Moll (shopping mall) at Volgograd, Russia near the Volga River. She was taken to a disused railway line next to the river, where her abductors tried to torture her. A fisherman on the shore yelled at them resulting in her abductors throwing her into the river and ran away. The fishermen grabbed her just in time and took her to his close by home. The elderly couple were delighted to feed the child and dressed her in their own children's packed away clothes. Their physician guessed the child's age at eight to nine months at the time. The physician suggested that they bring her back in six months for a further psychological examination as she characterized early symptoms of a mental illness disorder that possibly could affect her thinking process and disrupt her ability to function.[67] The couple took care of the child, a child they called Devanna after the Russian Goddess of the Hunt.

A Handful

Little Devanna was more than a handful for the Volkovs. They often complained to their own married children about her constant shaking, running with hands flapping in the breeze, and constant noise. "Iz-pod kontrolya demon, pozhaluysta, pomogite nam (out-of-control demon, please help us?), they asked their children. Their own children could not take Devanna as they had large families of their own, and they realized that Devanna's behavior would require a great deal of supervision.

When Mr. Volkov suffered and passed from a heart attack, Mrs. Volkov passed two weeks later, and the cute 2 year old Devanna was placed in a dyetskii dom (children's home).[68] The Volkov children believed that Devanna's behavior was one of the causal factors leading to the death of their parents. Not only was Devanna full of energy, but it seemed that she touched herself all the time. At the home, she was diagnosed with Attention-deficit/hyperactivity disorder (ADHD).[2] Compared with

---

[2] It is conceivable that Devanna's mama couldn't handle the out-of-control girl, and left her in stroller for the taking.

most children of the same age, little Devanna had difficulty with attention, impulsive behavior, and hyperactivity.[69]

During a careprovider's examination of the child, it was believed that Devanna was masturbating. While being examined, she punched the care provider in the nose and provided a babble laugh to go with her huge smile. Needless to say, Devanna was highly manipulative with her eyes and her little babble smile and calculating as it appeared that she chose who and when to behave like a demon child.

Adapted American Family

Devanna was adapted by the McDaniels before she reached 3 years of age by a happy Irish couple who lived in Iowa City, Iowa. They had two children of their own, one of each, whom they had adapted and felt that Devanna would round out the family into total happiness. However, they had no idea what they were getting into by any measure of the imagination. Yet, they decided to keep her name Devanna Volkov, but they were not aware how she came by that name nor did they care. Just for the record, Volkov refers to wolf and Devanna would live up to her name sake. The babbling smiles emanating from this marvelous child could not be ignored. Off they went to Iowa for what was hoped to be an amazing family life with their very own predator.

Devanna Killed Child of Her Adapted Family

It wasn't long before Devanna, 'accidently' killed her new family's youngest son. Together they were playing in the bathtub when Devanna turned on the hot water. Both children laughed and it appeared that they were having the time of their life. Soaking wet, Devanna jumped from the tab, plugged in an electrical cord she had seen in the sink cabinet and pitched it in the tub next to the little boy. Her tears spoke of the pain in her three year old heart, or at least that is what her providers were lead to believe when they entered the bathroom. During the funeral for the grieving parents, Devanna alone with the grandmother of the boy in the church rectory attacked her and bite her ear so hard that it was still in the mouth of Devanna when help arrived. Now her new parents finally realized what they were up against - a challenging obstruction better known as a brick wall.

The McDaniel Family

Since the passing of their youngest son, the McDaniel family's happiness turned toxic. Love was gone among the McDaniels but they tried hard to smile at Devanna and the others. Little Sadie McDaniel was told never to be alone with Devanna and the child obeyed, but did not understand why. She was desperately sad that her brother was no longer in her home. Late at night, Sadie's mother herd gurgling sounds from the bathroom. She jumped from bed and opened the bathroom door. Sadie was naked and laying on the floor. Hovering over her was Devanna whose fingers were inside the girl. Devanna showed no concern that Sadie's mother was suddenly present and reaching for Devanna's hands. Devanna slapped Mrs. McDaniel and her bubble laugh spread across her face. Standing now, she continued to kick the both of them and little Sadie's body responded with some blood. Mr. McDaniel hearing the commotion entered the bathroom and grabbed Devanna whose legs continued to kick despite her being held in the air. Her screams were truly paralyzing as was the laughter coming from this five year old child. Finally, Mrs. McDaniel sat on top of Devanna.

Iowa City's Department of Social Services

The McDaniels attempted to return Devanna to the children's home, but were informed that it wasn't possible because of the time lapse. On the advice of a neighbor, they contacted Iowa City's Department of Social Services (DSS) and after several interviews and the signing of numerous papers, DSS accepted the Devanna Volkov. It took less than two months for DSS to realize that the previous diagnose was correct: Devanna suffered from Attention-deficit/hyperactivity disorder (ADHD) resulting in difficulty with attention, extreme impulsive behavior, and hyperactivity. But two new diagnoses were added, she characterized antisocial personality disorder (ASPD), and she is a predator. How it was missed earlier is anybody's guess, yet, she had characterized behavior reflective of ASPD since birth and what some might call demonic possession. She was apparently born with both predispositions among others including the impulse to take the life of living things. Nonetheless, Devanna had few emotions especially about hurting others. When she did display emotions, it arose from her manipulation techniques when caught in deviant behavior. Her emotions also arose like a tsunami providing an astonishing euphoric feeling shouting through her veins when she attacked prey especially when her prey was dying – not dead mind you, but dying.

The McDaniels were advised to request aid which they did and the child was taken into custody by the Mercy Iowa City Behavioral Health Clinic for an assessment and observation. Her stay lasted only a week once careproviders caught Devanna hovering over a child, with her hands around the child's throat. She wouldn't let go as the careproviders struggled to release her hands. Too late! Of course, they were too late, Devanna knew the ceremony of death. The child died. After evaluating the evidence, a judge in chambers, directed that Devanna be remanded to Central Iowa Juvenile Detention Center.

10 Year Old Devanna

Her wide face and stocky build made Devanna appear to be older than 10 years old, and the extra padding of early childhood is visible under the detention center's uniform of a baggy green t-shirt and sweatpants. Her hands are red and chapped from the facility's allotted soap, dispensed from industrial-sized plastic jugs in the group shower. Her head is shaved down to a light fuzz; if she weren't sitting in the girls' unit, she might easily be mistaken for a boy. Everywhere you look, the signs of sexual assault, pregnancy, and other unique needs are obviously overlooked by a cursory and underfunded system.[70] Poor physical and mental health also emerges from the girls in this locked down facility, and there are tattletale gawks streaming below their eyes of sex trafficking among other decadent experiences.

Some girls in the room are engaged in an activity intended to help them bond with one another. The other girls, talk with one another about the drama between girls in high school, but Devanna keeps mostly to herself, chiming in at one point to tell them, "I'm not even in high school, yet." Devanna along with six other girls are crowded onto benches nailed to the metal table frame in the center of the room.

Update

Two months after Devanna was admitted to Central Iowa Juvenile Detention Center she was housed with another young girl, Elinor, who knew one of Devanna's victims. Elinor went out of her way to befriend Devanna so much so that the two of them were inseparable. Directly after lights out, Devanna was standing apparently ready to attack Elinor. But Elinor beat her to the attack and stabbed Devanna in the face 38 times with a kitchen fork smuggled into the facility by Elinor's mother.

Part III Fake Struggles
Chapter 8 Genocide and Demonic Possession in Guatemala

Overview

Genocide is a consequence of power, greed, racism, and censorship by perpetrators, which can include the dictators of the world.[71] When genocide is called by its other name, usually demonic possession becomes part of that adjective. Not necessarily possession by the perpetrators but the victims. This is an account of precisely that – the demonic possession of 7 year old Valeria Flores. She and her 10 year old fragile sister, Luciana both of Mayan descent. They lived in the small village of Malacatán, Guatemala close to the border crossover village of El Carmen with their grandparents the Pérezs. Their native language is Yucatec Maya but they also spoke Spanish and English similar to many educated Guatemalans like their father.

Both children were brutally tortured and violently raped by soldiers. Those soldiers raped and killed their grandmother while the children watched in horror. Afterwards, for 7 years, they were forced to serve as soldiers and sex slaves. They were injected with cocaine to curb their inhibitions towards the 'orders' of their masters during that 7 year period. Some of those 'orders' directed their children soldiers to commit atrocities such as killing the parents and their children of other captured persons who refused to be trained to kill for the army. They were all trained to assault, kill, and torch the villages they once called home without hesitation. Like mindless insects, they obeyed their superiors in all matters including sex and murder.

Her Fake and Real Struggle

In Valeria's mind, her fake struggle is cored in vengeance and payback. In reality, tattooed in her generics there remains no struggle at all, even as a sex slave and a child soldier. Her inclination or possession by the visible child demon, el Sombrerón since or probably before birth was obviously connected to her corrupt behavior. Her behavioral decisions very much matched John Wayne Gacy and Ted Bundy. But it might be more appropriate to suggest that the fiend in her head painted a more disturbing predator than Gacy and Bundy, let's try Pedro Alonzo Lopez who killed over 300 people in South America.[72]

Family Ties

Oddly enough, both Valeria and Luciana Flores were born on May 7th but four years apart. Valeria is fair, slight, and parades her sparking blue eyes despite both parents who are of Mayan descent. Luciana similar to most other Mayan children has an olive complexion, is a little overweight, and hosts dead brown eyes.

Valeria was treated differently than Luciana by most everybody and not necessarily because of Valeria's hostile personality contrasted to Luciana's low keyed and pleasant personality. Valeria loved drama, spontaneity, and exaggerated behavior while Luciana spoke less often and her behavior was predictable.

Their Father (U yuum)

There was talk that Valeria's father was an unknown Australian and Luciana's father was a local Mayan. But that accusation had little supporting evidence other than the appearance of both children. Their mother, an extremely attractive and fit woman, remained a cocaine user and alcoholic until the day she died. She was deeply religious and a devoted parent or at least devoted as long as she was observed. Their father assuming you accept the notion that the same individual fathered both children was also deeply religious yet his violent aggressive behavior was ignored by Luciana yet celebrated by Valeria. He had attended Santa Ana College in San Pedro Sacatepéquez, Guatemala and presently was a psychologist in a human resource department of a Brazilian corporation situated in San Marcos. He traveled to Mexico City and many cities in South America sometimes more than three weeks of every four. When at home, he would often instruct the girls how to use his computer for various searches. His aim was to teach them how to be independent and better learn their culture and their language.

Luciana tried hard to please him, but Valeria possessed a natural talent in learning about website searches despite her young age. Luciana never resented Valeria's abilities, and never tried to compete with her about anything. Valeria on the other hand, held feelings of jealousy with her sister and often lashed out and became aggressive toward her, when nothing was done to provoke such a strong reaction from Valeria.

Mayan Spirituality

Although majority of the Mayan population remains true to the Roman Catholic Church, mixed in with Evangelical Christianity, and a smaller Jewish and Muslim population has one mosque in Guatemala City. The Flores girls were excited about spirituality and helped their father learn about their extended family and their origins. They learned that Mayan spirituality consisting of pre-Columbian religious practices and a cosmology venerated natural phenomena, which includes rivers, mountains, and caves.[73]

The Flore ancestors were in workers of the temples built by the Mayan civilizations to mimic mountains and were constructed with a perfect alignment

with compass directions. The Flores girls found that finding very electrifying and they bragged to their friends about their ancestors. The core of Mayan religion is the belief describing everything in this world contains k'uh, or sacredness. K'uh and k'uhul, are similar terms used to explain the spirituality of all inanimate and animate things, and describe the most divine life force of existence.[74]

The point is that the stubbornness of evil spirits who breached a nun and took her to hell[3] continues to mount attacks upon the righteous and the foolish, and derives its

---

[3] They are exhibited at the Chartres Cathedral in France (see photo).

earthly powers in the highlands of Guatemala.[75] Since evil spirits were never provided a freewill, they can only pursue one course of action – destruction.

To better understand the thoughts of wicked evil behavior in Guatemala consider that during the civil war the systematic genocide of approximately 200,000 Guatemalan men, women, and children included 40,000 persons who "disappeared."[4] The Flores family was delighted that they were not part of that count, but didn't comment about it to anyone. Valeria found that to be a hard commitment and did her best to keep her mouth shut, but on a few occasions she couldn't resist her pride. Besides, she was killing the person she told about her heritage, so she felt that didn't count. Nonetheless, the Commission for Historical Clarification concluded that the beginning of the violence in Guatemala was the result of racist and exclusionary national policies, making it impossible for the state to achieve a social consensus.[76]

---

[4] Among others, Guatemala's chief of national police and the country's top anti-drugs official were arrested over links to drug trafficking while others were arrested for the massacre of Maya Ixil people.[4]

Evil Visited Upon the Flore Sisters

On their short walk from their preparatory school at Santa Lucia School Colegio in Malacatán to the home of their grandparents, Valeria, the six year old, said, "Yaan jump'éel extraña sensación iik" (there's a strange feeling in the air). And then she repeated herself in Spanish, "Hay un sentimiento extraño en el aire."

"Mantats' ocurrió a ba'alo'ob jela'antak wíits'ine'" (You always come up with strange stuff, little sister), was Luciana's reply.

"Chéen taan a in yáakunaj" (Just love me), Valeria said and again repeated herself in Spanish, "Solo Amame" as she slowed her pace to a sudden halt. Her big blue eyes were now focused on her big sister searching for some recognition of her thoughts.

Instead, Luciana's message and tone were far different than her usual manner annoying little Valeria. "Teech juntúul paal mimado," (you're a spoiled child) said she. Luciana added in a descending tone in English, "And don't throw a temper tantrum, little sister or the devil will get you." Luciana added with a point, "Look, there's our ilé baba àgbà" (grandparent's home).

True, Valeria threw temper tantrums, but only when those tantrums would bring her closer to whatever goal she had in mind, at the time.

Luciana was suddenly on the ground apparently the victim of a drop attack.[5] Looking up into her little sister's blue eyes which were fixated on Luciana, "Mina'an ba'ax in k'áaj u beetikten, in pool táan puesta" (I don't care what you do to me, my mind is set).

Luciana could feel her body crumpling into the earth but rather than say she was sorry to Valeria, she said nothing with her lips turned in over her spiteful face. As for Valeria, she decided that when get to their grandma's house, she would use her computer to search for the definition of 'spoiled child.'

Soldiers Appeared

At that precise moment when Luciana dropped, she felt it was all over for her. A hand of a soldier grabbed her helping her to stand. Unfortunately, this was not a meritorious moment for her or for Valeria. Three

---

[5] Injury is a common consequence of drop attacks. In France the condition has been called 'maladies de genius bleus' (sickness of the blue knees) because patients with drop attacks so often fall down on their knees.

government soldiers began their systematic torture of the two sisters. First, with hand slaps and then they used their fists. They didn't brother removing the clothes of the girls, but ripped the essential pieces off to fulfill their mission of sexual satisfaction, with every part of the girls' bodies.

Luciana cried and wailed. Valeria laughed and made fun of the soldiers no matter how hard they tortured her. Their grandmother appeared from nowhere, and cussed at the soldiers. She was violently raped and the girls were forced to watch. Then, one of the soldiers pulled his weapon from his holster, and put the weapon in Luciana's hand. "Shoot your girlfriend," said he in English.

When she refused, another soldier withdrew his knife and stabbed Luciana. Turning his attention to Valeria, that's when gunshots were heard and the soldiers quickly withdrew from their path of destruction. It was one of their own officers who chased them down and killed one of them while the other two carried the girls to their hidden camp. Luciana's blood was all over the soldier but he didn't seem to mine.

Sex Slaves and Murder

Even before Luciana's wounds healed, both she and Valeria were injected with a combination of drugs - an oxycodone (a high and sedative effect), Soma (muscle relaxant), and Xanax (crosses the blood brain barrier the fastest – producing a euphoric affect). This combination of drugs is known as The Holy Trinity of drugs.[77] The purpose of those injections were designed to make the victims comply with even the ugliest of demands and wishes of their owners. But also to keep the girls awake – like zombies.

Luciana became pregnant about two weeks later, 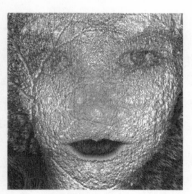 and when the child was born, both mother and child continued to please their masters. Valeria, despite her age, seemed to relish the attention of her masters through her enormous energy and encouraging attitude toward them, she couldn't get enough of anything regardless if it were torture, sex, or the murder of others. Some of those others included other captured children and their family members, if any of those children refused to submit to their masters. By the time she was 12, is was estimated that she was responsible for 40 or 45 murders and 10 villages torched.[78] Because of her proficiency in the field, she had a lot of freedom in comparison to most slaves. Yet because she was so free with her emotions, her behavior, and her acceptance of demands, she was a second choice to Luciana by their masters. Then, as if the sky lit up as both the strongest and wittiest demons descended upon Valeria, she literally raped her sister with a machete until she was dead. She made no attempt to wipe Luciana's blood from her own face.

Sweet Sixteen and Cyber Breaches

As Valeria's sweet sixteen birthday approached, she had worked hard to free herself of the massive army of black shadows in her mind which knocked her back to her previous world of decadent foul behavior. Or so she convinced herself of that fact, despite her cyber searches and penetrations into various official sites such as the Guatemala government and its military websites. It took some searches, but she eventually found a ten year old record of the Guatemalan officer who shot a soldier and chased after two others. Those records said nothing of the rape and murder of her grandmother nor did it say anything about the two young girls who were raped and taken as sex slaves. She intensified her cyber searches to learn the locations of the two soldiers. It took some time, but she learned that they were both convalescing from a fire bomb attack at the same military hospital.

An opportunity arose to aid the wounded and elderly populations of her home country – Guatemala. Before being assigned to the military hospital as a volunteer, she had a month's training. Her computer cyber skills paid off and now, she was at the specific military hospital where the two wounded soldiers were being treated.

She won the hospital staff and the two soldiers over with her charm and her skills. All the while her insides were turning upside down every time she viewed and spoke to the two soldiers who tortured and raped her and her sister and killed her grandmother. She knew she had to be patient and not display her real mission until the rest of her plan were in place.

She had learned online that those soldiers administered the Holy Trinity to her and her sister and she wanted to be certain that she had an ample supply of similar medications for them. Timing was everything and she was prepared to punish her offenders after the dinner hour and all through the night. After a few weeks on the job, she checked out of work early, but never left the center. She hid in a maintenance closet next to the room of the soldiers. She was prepared to help them severely pay for their sins in a like manner in which they sinned. The bat in her hand was her punishing instrument of choice and the Holy Trinity was an accomplice to her strategy. She pinned an official sign on the door notifying hospital staff passerbyers that the patients were not to be disturbed due to some complications. The duplicated signature of the hospital's chief administrator was appropriately signed at the bottom of the note. She knew that the hospital's chief administrator was not in the hospital that evening, and when not on the premises was not to be disturbed.

Upon entering the room of the two soldiers, she quickly injected both soldiers with an overdose of the Holy Trinity. She turned them over on their stomachs, and opened the ties to their medical capes. The bat was used to penetrate each of them, and the end of the bat was pushed into each of the mouths of the soldiers. Needles as painful as raw cactus were forced into each of their backs until the pain could not be controlled by the injected medication. More needles were pushed through their lips and cheeks from inside their mouths while small piece of wood held their mouths open.

She held each of their face up at a time and asked, "You remember me. I was one of the children you tortured and raped ten years ago." In the morning, Valeria left two dead bodies in the room and blended in with the hospital's morning routine. She remained as a volunteer for a few weeks after things settled down. It was believed that another soldier held a bitter vendetta against the two murdered soldiers. He was aided by his new hospital nurse lover and her body was discovered in a maintenance closet on the same floor as the murdered soldiers. Valeria had, indeed, engineered all the essential components necessary to take the lives of the soldiers but also to cast the blame of their murder on another soldier through her website skills.

Chapter Nine: The Trigger and the Bullet in New Orleans

Overview of Dominque Durand and Her Fake Struggle

Dominque (which means belonging to the Lord) Durand is a highly intelligent and wealthy girl who possesses an appetite for criminally violent behavior. The only way towards fulfillment of her emptiness relies on

one feast – killing. And she is not particular about her prey nor does she require to live in their shadow. She lives for the moment and right now, she's 18, but her violence apparently started 'before' birth.

She uses people as if they were her personal property. Her madness for murder isn't about personal fulfillment, but rather she kills because it's God's will. In her environment she responds without hesitation unless she is 'setting up' her victim for a final assault. And sometimes, after killing her prey, she often ate some of their body parts like a famished dog and sometimes she drained her victims of their vital fluids.[79] You might say, Dominique is highly manipulative, has no fear, and uses her body as her lethal weapon. How can she be sorry for her murders when it is the will of God, or so she believed?

To accomplice her goal, her method is quick and toxic going for the jugular, although she didn't know the name of what she grabbed and squeezed on for dear life until Nicole Oberly in 7th grade, explained it to her.

Presently, she works as a tour guide at The New Orleans Museum of Art and lives with Nicole Oberly in the Lakeview neighborhood of New Orleans. The museum is about a 15 minute subway ride from their apartment on the corner of Mouton and Colbert Streets home. Nicole is a student at Delgado Community College located across the street from the New Orleans Museum of Art. They met in 7th grade as you already know and since that time they have been inseparable. Here's what you need to know: Dominque has difficulty in making decisions, and is totally helpless without Nicole's direction. She has no self-reliance other than an urgent drive to kill. Nicole attempted to control Dominque's urges when it comes to deliberate and brutal murder. One way to understand their relationship is that Nicole is the trigger and Dominque is the bullet.

Natives of New Orleans

Currently, although Nicole was born in New Orleans, Dominique felt as much a native of New Orleans as Nicole. In high school they were locker neighbors and study-buddies at Benjamin Franklin High School.[6] They were both cheerleaders and adored by most of the guys on the sports' teams but none of them understood why neither girl wanted to date the athletes or anyone for that matter.

They knew better than to call them 'lesbians,' because one of the toughest boys on the high school football team did, and Dominique beat him so quickly and so badly that everyone kept their distance from her and Nicole. The beaten football player, in an attempt to regain his reputation tried to save himself by broadcasting that at the time of his beating, he was on medication. He

---

[6] Benjamin Franklin High School is a charter high school and a magnet high school in New Orleans, Louisiana. Commonly nicknamed "Franklin" or "Ben Franklin", the school was founded in 1957 as a school for gifted children and these girls are gifted with wealthy families, striking looks, and huge IQs.

should have been thankful that Dominique didn't kill him, but no one at Benjamin Franklin High School knew of the deadly activities of the girls. Well, not the girls, just Dominique while Nicole was a submissive servant to Dominique and secretly, Nicole couldn't live without the love of her life who never felt the 'love' returned.

Oh, there were two exceptions about who knew of  Dominique's predatory life style: the school counselor and the now strangely deceased psychology teacher and his family. Nicole was only an observer to most of Dominique's violence, yet she is included in the understanding that they were both prompts of the brutal truths of ancient demons who hold the rank of chief female predators and who always would surface for the sacrifice no matter how small or how large the sacrifice.

Overview of Dominique Durand's Wealthy Family

Her father was a Scottish noblemen who lived on the Isle of Islay also known as Whiskey Island, off the west coast of Scotland. He owned two distilleries and lived in an ancient castle that was completely refinished to suit his tastes. Her wealthy mother was from Coulombiers, a commune in Poitou, France about ninety minutes to La Rochelle situated on the Bay of Biscay and the Celtic Sea. Her mother left her father when he humiliated her and called her an adulteress in the courtroom during a property dispute over the 4,000 (about 6.5 square miles) acers owned by her family. She immediately took Dominique to New Orleans and enrolled her in 7th grade. Both of Dominque's sisters were already in the American university system - Palatine was in her 3rd year at Butler and Genevieve in her second year at the University of North Carolina. Both sisters lived on their respective campuses. Her mother purchased and operated an artists' shop in the French Quarter. She named renamed it to 'Art, Frames and Supplies.'

Nicole Oberly's Childhood Experiences

Nicole Oberly was born and raised in New

Orleans by her Louisiana French family. She had only one brother who is gay. Her father was a plumber and her mother took care of the home and the children. Nicole regarded herself as a visionary and not as a demoniac, something many of her family members talked about. Seems demoniac takeovers and evil spirits are always part of the New Orleans culture and history. As a child and a teenager, she felt that violence was a poor response, no matter the circumstance. More specifically, she would not employ violence herself but might approve the use of violence under certain circumstances. She understood that she always possessed an ability to influence others in many ways. For example, when she was three, she closed her eyes and wished her brother would pop his playmate at daycare. He did. She was amazed and experimented on others to see if they were driven by her thoughts, too.

Although her thoughts were sometimes blurry and the end result confused the behavior of some of her alleged victims. She didn't comprehend why some individuals, sort'a followed her thoughts while others didn't. She couldn't understand why her intended behavior happened in a different way than she intended it to happen. For instance, at the food store with her brother they were standing in line to pay for some candy. A rude man also waiting to pay for his items made fun of her brother. She willed that the woman standing behind the rude man, drop the frozen turkey she was carrying on his foot. It didn't happen. But when the rude man paid for his items, the boy who was bagging for the cashier, dropped the rude man's bag on his foot.

Nicole, when 5 years old, tried to 'will' her church priest (her family was Catholic) to shudder during his sermon, something he had never done as long as she would remember. He didn't. Now, Nicole was totally confused. At first, she was impatient with her learning about her abilities. At 7, when not in school or performing house chores, she spent hours in her bedroom going over and over her past happenings in an attempt to learn what worked and what didn't work. She never confided with anyone for fear that they would call her a witch. She had seen some children avoided and humiliated when others provided them the title of witch for behavior that didn't conform to other children. Witches, Voodoo and New Orleans are very much connected in the minds of many. In fact, the liturgical language particularly of Voodoo was Louisiana Creole, but Nicole spoke the language of her heritage known as Louisiana French as her family came from a long line to the French colonists.

Nicole's Computer Searches and Mind Control

To aid her in a quest to understand and control her ability to will others, she turned to her computer for answers. Be clear, she didn't have one at 8 years of age, so she 'willed' her mother to get her one on the pretense of helping her through grade school. Her computer searches were in vain for most part. She keyed in ideas such as willing people, power over people, mind control, and numerous other combinations including meditation. Luckily, her computer has a spell check linked to its keyed in items, saving her hours in plugging in her requests. Yes, she tried to 'will' the computer to work for her, with no luck – least she tried! She came across wish-fulfillment but couldn't grasp its full meaning. It read, "wish-fulfillment: As an advanced meditator wishes anything, it will be provided by the so-called unified field and without recourse to ordinary, natural principles."[80]

The article went on to say that as human-beings have secret desires and something about super powers are a lie and a fool's dream. Although her 9 year old mind didn't accept or truly understand what she read, it did convince her that she was on the right track in the sense that real magic and the miracles are performed in a quiet way. "Kind of like the stuff the best witches are dealing with…"

'Willing' Power and Witches

"There it is – people with powers, that others don't have, are witches," she whispered to herself. Another article related to her as she understood it, that witches had magic or the power to control minds or mental manipulation influencing their thoughts and actions.[81] "So, yippy, I could be a witch and will others not to call me a witch!" She finally figured out her position in this world sandwiching her into the chills. The article read that the power to exert control over the mind of others is not necessarily rare, but it is an uncertain form of magic. She decided using the article as a guide that her willing power as it were can deprive a person of free will and therefore she, Nicole Oberly, is demon from the hot rocks of hell – she's evil! "Naaa," she whispered to herself. "I'm just an angel longing for chaos."

Nicole had spent hours in her room on her computer because there were sentences and words utilized she did not understand – after all, she was only 10 years old. The significance of her age suggests that over the past few years, Nicole researched the internet and practiced her willing powers.

Nicole's Words are Magic

Nicole learned that she when she spoke the words, individuals were more likely to follow her words, but they had to hear them. That meant she had to be close to the individual whom she was 'willing,' and other should not hear her willing as they too might respond accordingly. She also learned that by speaking the words, violence by others was a possible outcome. She possessed the power of mind control through her words.

To test this idea, as she sat next to her favorite uncle during Sunday dinner, she whispered into his ear to kill her aunt with a knife. Nicole and her little brother as well as her mother and father sat in horror as her uncle completed his mission. They were all crying in disbelief, yet Nicole thought it was very very Gucci. She would save her smiles until she went to her room after the police left.

Dominique and Nicole in 7th Grade

They were assigned to each other in chemistry class after Nicole spoke to her and sat down. There was something odd about the pairing by chemistry teacher who seemed to hesitate while assigning the girls. The teacher seemed fixated on Nicole's expressions for some reason or another. While the girls moved from the desks to the chemistry tables, Nicole seemed to notice the dusky fire gleaming in Dominique's eyes. "You're going to be my best friend ever," whispered Nicole to Dominque. Dominque felt a pull to Nicole similar to magnet's response to earthy materials. They smiled at each other. Strange, Dominque thought, she didn't feel an urge to harm Nicole. After class throughout the week, the two girls were together talking. Dominque tried hard to please Nicole, although she didn't know why and Nicole sat back and watched Dominque's very moment and listened to every word she said about her life as she spilled the beans.

Dominique Spills the Beans

She told Nicole as they sat under a cherry tree at the middle school yard that she didn't know that she "was bad. I love music and wear an earpiece listening to Dua Lipa and Lady Gaga."

"Yeah, I see it in your ear. What kind is it?"

"It's like a Sony Bluetooth. Took it from a girl I destroyed."

She went on to tell Nicole that when she was younger like 3 years old, she attacked her brother and hurt him bad. Her parents were furious with her. Two weeks later, she killed their cocker spaniel dog, Sandy and said it was an accident. She killed their new puppy after it was in the family for a week. She lifted the pup into a garbage can and explained with dazzling eyes that the 'kill' was exciting. She told her mom that she saw some boys jump their fence and "hurt our puppy." She thought about attacking her parents and decided that she would wait until she was older. The more Nicole prompted her, the more Dominique devolved her ruthless tales.

At five or earlier, she wasn't sure, she touched herself whenever she could and thought how great it felt, but attacking things felt better and made a place for her in her "little world." She was needed! Somewhere around 6, she believed that she was fulfilling God's mission to attack and kill the evil things of the world which was anybody living a sinful life or not. In part, she decided on this justification of her killing at church when the priest preached from the bible that a person can't see heaven until they die. So she decided to help them see heaven sooner.

At 8 years of age, she would walk outside her neighborhood and track down animals to kill. Once, a young boy ran over on her on his bike as she was walking on the sidewalk. She searched the neighborhood and found his home. She waited for him one day in his garage, the door was open giving her the impression that his parents were out. His bike was missing and assumed he would be coming home soon. He did. And she bitterly attacked him faster than he could yell. His murder didn't take long. Her insides "were so happy. God wanted that bad boy dead to judge him up there so I drained him of stupid fluids right there in the garage with my mouth and hands."

Sisters Learned of Father's Humiliation of Their Mother

Dominque explained with some prompting by Nicole that when Palatine, her sister, learned of her father's humiliation tactics in court which included her mom being an adulteress suggesting that her and her sisters were fathered by different men, she gathered both her sisters, Genevieve and Dominque, and flew to his island paradise near Scotland. In their attempt to discuss with him his humiliation of their mother, his bodyguards stepped in. Without so much as a wink, 10 year old Dominique, attacked their father like a lighting stick to the face and ripped out one eye and seriously damaged the other one. Her attack was so quick and so precise that her sisters and his bodyguards were in shock. She turned to one of his bodyguards and with the accuracy of trained killer, ruthlessly attacked him. The two sisters taking their lead from little Dominique attacked the other guards. The girls took their father's body, and dropped him into a water hole in a cave on the island and flew home.

Dominique's Exorcism

Upon their return to New Orleans, they informed their mother that Dominique must be possessed by an evil spirit. Dominique told Nicole that "oh they thought that an exorcism was the way to rid me of my demons, but I tricked them into believing that it worked and hunted down the two guys who performed the exorcism and wacked them both to pieces."

Nicole Provided Information on Prey and a Serial Killer

As the days and months past, the two BFFs were very active. Nicole's computer stalked various individuals she didn't like or those who took issue with her such as her stepfather and her second grade teacher. She provided the time and place for Dominque to attack these individuals as well as others.

Part of Nicole's hunt, she visited the New Orleans Public Library where she would sit for a few hours observing the comings and goings of various people especially students. She would prepare a hit list consisting of names, addresses, and cell photos for Dominque. One fear Nicole had was what would happen if Dominque became bored or started to think for herself. Could Nicole become a target? She had to keep her busy.

Nicole provide Dominque with further descriptions of thugs and serial killers in the New Orleans. The advantage of New Orleans was that there were many murders committed and a high percentage of them were never reported let alone investigated unless it was a bar fight or in the home of an unhappy couple. In one case, girls were disappearing rapidly in the area and the newspapers said that a serial killer was on the loose.[82] Nicole through her hacking skills was able to hack into police systems and learned of three persons of 'interest' for those crimes. She narrowed it down to one twenty-one year old man, Neal Tumbles. He lived in the Quarter with his elderly mother. Nicole was able to get a blueprint of some of his activities. His residence was a 20 minute subway ride for the girls. Yes, Nicole thought they should go together. At the time they were both 14 years old and would wander around the Quarter after Dominque performed her duty to God and to Nicole.

Gaining access to Tumbles' home was easy before he came home from work. His mother invited the girls in on the expectation that her son has a romantic thing for one of the girls. When police arrived at the scene of the brutal double homicide, both corpuses were drained of their bodily fluids and most of it remained on the floor. The forensic officer screeched his head looking at one of the officers, "No one touched these fluids, right? There seems to be a lot missing." In his home the authorities discovered an arsenal of weapons that could be characterized as a serial killer's kill kit. On the wall, were photos obvisouly taken by a cell that represented a hit list of 10 girls whom he would attack, but now would never have a chance. Unbeknown by the cops, one of the photos was of Dominque.

As Police Neared Dominque

As police investigations in and around New Orleans seemed to near Dominque, Nicole went to work on her computer. She had to offer Dominque a way out if it came to an arrest. The complexity of spirit possession as a psychological and psychopathological behavior necessitates a personal subconscious motivation, but Dominque lacked a subconscious. Nicole is the closest representation of a subconscious for Dominque.

Nicole the Black Hat Hacker

A hacker could refer to anyone with technical skills who invades web sites. However, it typically refers to an individual like Nicole who uses her skills to achieve unauthorized access to systems or networks so as to commit or promote crimes.[83] In this case, to have Dominque carry out murder.

Nicole often utilized a 'brute force' cyberattack to obtain data she sought and it has a two sided goal for her – a hunt for prey and to keep Nicole safe from Dominque.[84] A brute force attack includes 'speculating' username and passwords to increase unapproved access to a framework.[7]

---

[7] Just for the record, the intent of the internet burglaries can determine the classification of those attackers as white, gray, or black hats.[7] White hat attackers burgled networks or PC systems to get weaknesses so as to boost the protection of those systems. Grey hat hackers are a blend of both black hat and white hat activities. Often, grey hat hackers seek vulnerabilities in a system without the owner's permission or knowledge. If issues are discovered, they will report

Nicole Finds Asylum for Dominque

Nicole did her homework and cyberhacked a number of web sites and concluded that panic disorder is the easiest fooler of all the mental disorders because a comprehensive evaluation by psychiatrists is centered in the answers of patients to questions asked by a physician regarding the patient's feelings, emotions, and behavior.[85]

Convincing Dominque of a new strategy is not even a concern for Nicole because Dominque submits to Nicole without hesitation in all matters except love and sexual relationships. Nicole's love for Dominque is one sided. Although Dominque loves Nicole but not enough to jump in bed with her. One of Dominque's fears was that if she kissed Nicole, she would turn her into a dragon. And the thought is always there for Nicole that if she pushed her into bed and Dominque was unhappy

---

them to the owner, sometimes requesting a small fee to fix the issue. Black hat hackers tend to have extensive knowledge about breaking into computer networks and can easily bypass security protocols. They can also write and insert malware, which is a method used to gain access to these systems. Black hatters can pursue cyber espionage, protest, or are addicted to the thrill of cybercrime, or like Nicole have a mission resulting in murder among other violent crimes.

about it – Nicole could find herself in a risky predicament.

Nicole's cyber hacking offered a strong argument to keep Dominque out of reach of police suspicion during their investigations. According to the news reports, a girl fitting Dominque's description was seen leaving two of the murders sites. Anyone fitting that description was under suspicion. New Orleans was now plagued with out of control and unsolved stranger murders and clearly Dominque was one of the culprits responsible for many of those murders. In fact, one headline at WWL-TV read "27 people have been killed in New Orleans through two months in 2020."[86]

"Why didn't you tell me before that I have panic… what?

"Panic attacks, dear girl. You don't, but you're going to pretend you do," said Nicole. "You need to provide cops with some understanding if they question you that you behave the way you do without them suspecting what you really are - a killing machine. Because, if you're suspected of a crime or arrested you would not necessarily fit the description of what you are."

Nicole paused and added, "Let's go over your lines until you actually sound like a young girl with a panic disorder."

Panic Attacks

"According to my (cyberhacking) research, these panic attacks typically begin suddenly, without warning.[87] They strike at any time no matter where you are," mentioned Nicole. "You have frequent attacks and you're doing your best to control them."

Nicole goes on to inform Dominque about the symptoms. She highlighted feeling of impending doom, fear of loss of control, and feeling of detachment. The greatest fear Nicole mentioned to Dominque is the intense fear that you'll have another panic attack at any time. For that reason, Nicole explained "You avoid crowds and other possible situations where those attacks might happen."

"Why do I need to know this?" she asked.

"Not just know, Sweetie, but a doctor will diagnose you as characterizing a panic disorder. When you're ready, I've made an appointment with a psychiatrist who is new to her profession so she'll follow the dots and end up with the right diagnose for you."

Appointment with the Psychiatrist

Dominque knew her lines but had to rehearse with Nicole many times. "Tell me again why I need to sound like a person with a mental illness?"

"Because of the brokenness of the system. They're looking for victims, too, that's the rhythm of life. If an arrest is made, the AG knows the chances of prison conviction is not as likely as confinement in a mental illness facility." At the end of the appointment with the psychiatrist, Dominque walked out of his office into the waiting area where Nicole patiently sat. Dominque was whipping blood from her lips. Nicole knew that Dominque killed the psychiatrist and her nurse. Quickly they entered exit door and climbed into Nicole's car. "Can't take you anywhere," she said with a laugh. "They asked me if I preferred girls or boys. I told them that they would do."

Nicole replied, "Sweetie, they were asking about your friend relationships not who you preferred to eliminate."

"Oh!"

Update

Eventually Dominque and Nicole moved out of New Orleans to New York City where the murder rate was higher than New Orleans. Nicole's thinking was that the chances of Dominque being apprehended were less likely than New Orleans. She was right about that.

Chapter 10: Greta the Gang Leader in Beverly Hills

Greta led her gang, The Bi'hes of several girls in the torture murder of Stella Albright, an up incoming Hollywood star at 16 years of age. Stella was caught in a lesbian love triangle, and while the gang tortured Stella,  Greta bit the victim's thighs and spit out some of her flesh on the victim's face. They burned what was left of Stella down at the Los Angeles River near Griffith Park at midnight.[88] This was hardly the first 'roast fest' for The Bi'hes, unlike other female gangs, this one is comprised of approximately 44 young, wealthy, Caucasian girls from Beverly Hills. Yet, to be on the level with the readers of this chapter, 12 of those gang members were actually servants of some of the girls. Last month, one of Greta's gang members refused to attack a girl who wouldn't complete gang initiation. The practice was common and generally consisted of attacking and raping a member of opposing female gangs such as the Bloodettes, a branch of the Latin Bloods. After all, the Bi'hes was family for its 40 some members and each of them completed their initiation to join up including the 12 servants.

Greta attacked and brutally pounded the gang member who refused to attack the girl. She pounded her face with a pipe while her girls cheered her on. Before she died, Greta bit off her nose. She turned on the other girl held by her members, and knifed her to death. She spit the nose of her now died gang member into the mouth of the girl and placed the pipe in the hand of her dead gang member. Before calling the cops, members of the Bi'hes, soaked both girls with gasoline and set them on fire. They cheered again. Then she called the cops on the cell of dead   gang member with a description of the two girls and blamed it on the Bloodettes. They fled the ally way near Barnsdall Art Park and disappeared into the wooded park area. Oh, by the way Greta had just turned 15, and was the youngest member of the Bi'hes.

Experts Would Say

Experts would say that Greta and probably her girls possess high callous and unemotional traits and therefore tend to join with antisocial and delinquent peers to commit crimes in groups.[89] High callous traits suggest being insensitive; indifferent; unsympathetic. As usual, the experts have a short vision of people like Greta and all of her girls. For one, they are not unemotional and insensitive. Torture and murder push their emotions to extreme levels of joy and accomplishment. Torture and killing are exciting activities that fill a void, relieve boredom, and in gangs, fortifies the bond or cohesion among the family (gang members). Individually, killers similar to Greta attack others at young ages suggesting a birth predisposition toward murder and torture, but let's say they weren't born evil – they are evil spirits with a human body.

Glen's (Greta's) Birth

Glen's mother was a famous Hollywood star appearing in several popular movies, and her father was equally popular. He extensively traveled, almost as much as his mother, to shot movies on the set in foreign countries including the UK and Mexico. Glen John Austin was secretly born behind closed doors since his mother was only dating her father at the time. Carrying her child was more than challenging because baby rarely stopped kicking and moving around inside her. Labor lasted several hours and it was almost as if the child did not want to leave mama's womb. He fought but lost, and apparently was bitter about it based on his fighting and crying once in the nurse's arms. She was not prepared for such a bitter child and handed baby over to his mother who held him tight with "Shhh, little one. Mama's got you." The physician ordered a quick injection to make the baby tranquil.

It would take four or five years before the Glen's mother and father would make their relationship public. In Glen's young life he described it as somewhat uneventful for a child from wealthy and nationally celebrated parents. The family had estates all over the world, but preferred their estates at Virginia Water in Surrey in the UK and Motu Tane, Bora Bora, French Polynesia (both considered to represent the most expensive properties on the planet).

At 3 Careproviders and Bodyguards

He continued to fuss and cry for many hours during the day and the night as you already have imagined. He later learned that he was a colic child. At 3 years of age, he punched her grandmother in the face when she laughed at his behavior. When disciplined by his careproviders, he punched them, too, and offered his typical hysterical laugh. Glen was drawing scrambled pictures of weapons: knifes, guns, arrow ends, and his parents weren't sure where he saw pictures of those items, but there they were. He was rough on his stuffed animals and other children if they were around.

Glen and his older step-sister on her father's side, Joanna, similar to most children from excessively wealthy and tolerated family members were both raised by highly paid and trained younger 'dodtees' (Glen's name for his careproviders, a few were in their teens) from the time they left their mother's womb, until Greta (his new name) entered prison at 16 years of age as a high risk serial killer. In addition to dodtees, both Glen and Joanna were under constant surveillance by women who never smiled, wore black slacks and button down shirts, and carried weapons on their belts. Glen called them shadows. Even when the children slept, shadows were outside their bedroom doors. The fear was that the children would be kidnapped and held for ransom. Later, Glen would learn they were bodyguards. Clearly, Glen's parents were never ever around not just because of their occupation demands but also because of Glen's out of control behavior.

Age 4 the Castle

Glen moved his careproviders' clothes, toothbrushes, and shoes to other rooms, within the large living complex he called home, and his careproviders called it 'The Castle.' Sometimes he would hide those items in the dishwasher, oven, and clothes dryer. Glen was greatly amused as they searched around the quarters for their belongings. There were times when he hid items in the garage, backyard, garbage containers, and stable. Steeling things from those individuals was a compulsion with him up to the time she arrived at prison.

Age 5 Christmas Week

During Christmas week, he took some presents from under the Christmas tree with different names of

190

them and fired them up in the garage. "That was incredible," he commented to no one and everyone. His dodtees and a few of his shadows tried to put out the fire after it started, and Glen found it amusing to yell "fire fire" as loud as he could.

They're screaming at each other about what to do, was also amusing for Glen. Joanna was coming over that morning in her pajamas and she arrived just in time to catch the screams, tears, and his snickers. Suddenly, when it was almost over, Glen's snickers turned to tears. When a dodtee asked about his tears, he said, "I didn't want Teddy [the stuffed bear she was holding] to catch fire." Then he pretended to be upset and out of control and struck dodtee with his teddy several times, until Joanna stopped him.

Glen's False Struggle and Evil

Glen continued to believe his struggle was over rejection and he was probably right about that because his conduct dictated to his careproviders and his family members that he lacked a conscious, was unpredictable, and was individually glorified by his corrupt and

191

destructive behavior. In reality, Glen's fetus was corrupted by spirit of evil and this demon would not let go of Glen probably even after his death.

On more than three occasions, without provocation, he attacked careproviders with screams, fists, and a biting mouth. On other occasions, he threw bottles and opened cans of Pepsi Cola at them and snickered the whole time.

Age 6

Glen possessed few if any personal boundaries, despite his sweet smile, and his dominant alpha-personality which was masked by a charismatic and dramatic nature. At home his dodtees more or less followed his lead despite her age. They feared him because of the dangerous actions he waged against them. For example, there was a pot of boiling water on the stove and Glen tried to splash it on one of the dodtees. The pot was too heavy and too hot for him to handle. He was six or 7 at that time. He dropped the pot, jumped, and cried. Glen said it was an accident. The next time boiling water was on the stove, he scooped a cupful from the pot, and pitched it at one of his careproviders.

Age 7

He waited till her dodtees particularly the older ones (in their early 20s) were asleep and entered one of their facilities. He lit up her blankets with a match and lighter fluid and quickly fled. After that the Dodtees insisted on locked doors to their quarters. As you can expect, some of the dodtees came and went but several stayed particularly after the primary home provider who handled all the finances for the home, gave them huge incentives to stay such as better health insurance, higher salaries, paid vacation's time, and actual paid vacations such as airline tickets and hotels. Once Glen's bodyguards (or shadows as Glen called them) discovered the incentives for dodtees, they requested similar benefits.

Age 8-9 Steeling Binges, Computer Searches and Feminine Activities

Joanna would search stores on her computer and see what others were saying about those stores. If the staff had complaints about being too aggressive with their customers, it was a no. If the staff according to visitors of those stores wrong that the staff was pleasant and respectful, it was a yes. Steeling binges with her little brother, Glen and constant companion entered girly stores and insisted that their 'shadows' remain outside. A few of Glen's loyal young dodtees accompanied them sometime.

They would steel jewelry, girls' clothes, and scarfs, some of which Glen would put around his neck and look in the mirror. He would strike different possesses and ask Joanna, "Am I cute?" He only stole girly things that looked good on him particularly if one of his dodtees remarked that he looked 'awesome.' He would slip shorts on over his shorts and check himself out in the mirror.

Joanna realized that Glen, at 8 liked what he saw in those girly stores and he tried on some of the outfits, for fun. But Joanna felt that she was with another girl, and later decided that Glen was trapped in a boy's body.

They were sneaky and confident in their shoplifting habits. What neither of the two of big shoplifters didn't know was that the shop keepers kept track of their theft activities, and sometimes added more money on top of the stolen merchandise for good luck, and reported their loses to Glen and Joana's careproviders who paid for the stolen merchandise. Joanna often witnessed Glen's change from cute and feminine to fireball. For example, the first time Joanna witnessed 'another' Glen was when a young person imitated Glen's walk in at one of the shopping malls. Glen tore into him as quick as lightening, and security officers and Joanna pulled him off the older boy. Fortunately, he, nor would his mother press charges against Glen.

Age 10

Around 10 years of age, the shoplifting continued as Glen and Joanna went on "stealing binges" to Walgreens, CVS, and Walmart, among other retailers, graduating eventually into the high-end retailers. Those retailers too were about five miles from their neighborhood, so loyal dodtees or shadows had to drive them. The dynamic duo ripped off large quantities of expensive lotions, perfume, and cosmetics. They gave a lot of the stolen goods to their dodtees and shadows. It wasn't about keeping the goods, it was about the sensation of theft that appealed to Glen more than Joanna.

Age 12 Conversations about Glen's Feminine

Joanna had some conversations with Glen when he was 12 years old about his 'feminine' ways. "Oh," said he, "I'm not sure about my body, but I know something is wrong."

Glen had some conversations with his dodtees over the next few months and his shadows at least those whom he didn't attack, who said the same thing to him. "Talk to your mother about how you feel."

He tried several times at least when she was around. Joanna tried too. No luck. And finally, Joanna said, "I searched the computer for gender change physicians with their own clinics that would work with you. I jumped into their computer systems and added you as a new patient referred by another doctor. I hacked his system, too, with your information. A dodtee will say she's your mother and I'll say I'm your sister – which of course I am. Your shadow will drive you to the clinic." Joanna also hacked into the doctor's website and provided a parent's approval for gender reassignment surgery. She told Glen that he has a surgical appointment with Dr. Gerald Monger at 3 tomorrow afternoon. Joanna and 12 year old Glen with his mother arrived on time and the doctor scheduled surgery at his clinic after a few more interviews including one with his craniofacial team.

His decision with Glen, Joanna, and Glen's (forged documents provided by Joanna) mother, would be to reduce the prominence of Glen's brow, reduce the prominence of his Adam's apple, adjust the jawline, and rhinoplasty to make the nose more feminine. The procedure would be conducted over several days and Joanna was present the entire time. The doctor wanted to meet Glen's mother probably because she was a celebrity and Joanna provided an appointment before the surgery. But, "She had to fly to Argentina for a movie shoot. She said she'd like you over to the house upon her return. She also said take care of my child."

Torture and Murder after Surgery of Surgeon and Nurse

Three weeks after surgery, 'Greta' revisited Monger's office complaining of a terrible inch under her chain. The doctor's nurse prescribed oxycodone for her in the waiting room. Greta was not happy with one prescription. "I need more over a longer period of time."

"Let me check with the doctor," was her reply.

"I'm with a patient," Monger said over the phone intercom.

Greta would have none of it. She stood, walked to the door and spoon the double office door lock. She turned to the nurse and silently and without so much as a rapid breath, killed her almost instantly with her hands. She touched her breast, "I should have some of these," Greta whispered to herself. Now she moved into the office of the doctor who was surprised to see her at the door. "I'm sorry, I'll be done in a second here." His naked female patient was sitting on the end of his exam table. Legs spread wide.

"Oh, so sorry I invaded your little party." With that, Greta the monster killed them both and moved back and forth between the two victims, punching, biting, and shoving his hand down his patent's throat. Blood was everywhere and on Greta, too. She wasn't able to carry his body on the table, but she did drag his nurse's broken body into the room. All three bodies were now lifeless, and on the floor. She compared the two girl's bodies to one another. Moving, swinging, and eating as she went along. Her feast lay before her, but first she celled Joanna and asked her to hack into the doctor's files and eliminate everything. "You mean your appointments, diagnosis, and surgery?"

"Yes, right away please."

"Are you at his office?" Joanna paused, and asked, "Did you....?"

"Yes, but this time there's three of them."

"When I'm done, I'll be right over."

For the rest of the day, Greta devoured the body parts she liked best starting with the breasts of both girls even though the nurse's breasts were very small. She did move one of mouth of one of the girls over the doctor's private part, and moved the girl's mouth biting it, and eventually, parts of it were in the bleeding mouth of the nurse. "Yeah," screamed Greta, and licked the nurse's mouth of all the blood on it. She made slits in each body, allowing their blood to drain all over the floor. She moved the surgeon's knife deep into the abdomen of each girl, and with her hands pulled out their stomachs, and intestines licking as she went along. Every so often she would comment, "Sweet," or "lit" (amazing), or "Yolo" (You only live once)."

"I'm so baked (tired), and she cupped her face on the girl's head that remained contacted to the body. She slept for maybe twenty minutes when her cell rang (military bugle music alarm). "Hey, it's Joanna. Let me in. I'm at the office door."

When Joanna came into the waiting area, she put the sign on the door that said they were closed and entered the surgeon's room, her eyes went wide. "Oh I see, you've been busy!" Before she leaned over in total fear for her own life this time, Joanna said, "Kiss me." Then she leaned over and whipped some of the blood from Greta's face and off her own lips with her hands and licked them with a false smile, and looked below her eyes.

Joanna noticed that the two bodies of girls were ripped open and some of their body parts were removed but she couldn't identify them among the other body parts on the floor. The doctor's zipper was open and through the blood, Joanna noticed that his private part was missing.

"She did it," Greta said pointing to one of the girls so I cut her insides out." And Greta opened the girl's mouth reaching for his penis and showed it to Joanna. "See, she's really the bi'he here. He sucks monkey nuts, no way for me. Humm, bi'he, I like that sound."

Joanna helped Greta wash the blood from her naked body and all the while observing Greta's eyes so as not to offend her. "Do you want me to wash, down her, too?

"Yes, please, because it's an itchy place." They found some of the nurse's street clothes in the closet, and of course they really didn't fit but there wasn't blood on them. Once both Joanna and Greta were ready, Greta grabbed her prescription orders and took some medications from the doctor's office windowed chest.

Age 13 Greta and Joanna Stay High Cruising For Drugs

This Dr. Jekyll and Mr. Hyde lifestyle drove Joanna crazy, but Greta thrived in the environment she created. Joanna asked an older girl, Brenda and her brother, Arnold, who lived in the neighborhood to include Greta and her in their weekly drives into the Boyle

Heights and East LA areas to buy their drugs. It became a regular routine for them over the months, and sometimes they got high together at one of their homes. A few times, Arnold made some series passes at Joanna and it was not taken lightly by Greta whose eyes widened quickly. "Stop that," Joanna said to the Arnold. "The last thing in this world if you wanna live is to piss off, Greta. And don't laugh about it please or we'll have to find other ways to get our drugs."

Brenda stepped in too, and told Arnold, "That's enough!" She knew like many other neighbors of Greta's penchant toward criminally violent behavior.

The serious money for them was appealing, but the friendship for Brenda with the two girls was more motivating for her otherwise she had to be in the company of Arnold. The girls sat in the back seat, and Brenda and Arnold sat in the front sit. He handled all the transactions for drugs. Joanna observed him closely wanting to learn the techniques of a buyer.

One time while the crew was waiting for Joanna to leave her home and join them, Arnold jumped into the back seat with Greta. She used her hands to make him happy while Brenda watched. Jumping into the vehicle, Joanna voiced, "That's the last time for this shit. She's 13 years old and I love her." Looking at Greta, "I'm sorry, sweet one, I don't have a dick, but you know I care."

"What? Twelve, holy shit!" said Arnold.

Looking at Brenda, "Why didn't you stop your brother?" Joanna asked with a squinted look.

"Greta told me to mind my own business, and I'm not going to get her pissed at me. I love her, too."

Joanna replied with, "Look," now staring into the eyes of Arnold, "If for some reason you ever disappoint Greta, she could give you your worst experience ever, right, Greta?"

Greta grinned. "I thought about ripping his dick out but knew you coming soon and we didn't want to be surrounded by blood."

Arnold quickly whipped the smile off his face and froze after Greta's comment.

"Sorry, sorry, sorry. It'll never happen again," he slowly said to Greta.

One time during their regular search for drugs, the vehicle was stopped by the police and when they the cops realized who Greta and Joanna were, one said, "Have a nice day, and don't speed."

Age 14 Greta and Her Gang

Greta knew which buttons to push when dealing with her dodtees. They knew that if they became an adversary, they would become subject to Greta's manipulation, torment, and random attacks which included putting an ice pick through the dodtee's car tires, steeling their mail, and making up stories about the targeted dodtee and possibly losing their job. But then there was torture and murder, too. A few times, she physically attacked dodtees with a knife, and after killing one, she demanded that her loyal dodtees hide the body. Joanna became aware of the loyal 'subjects,' and suggested that they, meaning Joanna and Greta and Greta's loyal dodtees take to the streets for fun. Once the dodtees were told that they would keep their benefits including their salaries, they agreed to anything Greta told them to do. Brenda and several other girls in the neighborhood would join them particularly after her brother said he was through with helping them buy drugs.

"We'll buy our own stuff and fun, too. What an awesome fam we have."

"Remember the name - Bi'hes. That's our gang name, Bi'hes."

"I love it," responded Joanna, "and you're our gang leader."

"But I'm only 14!"

"Not to worry, my love," said Joanna. "No one is better for the job. And everyone will listen to you."

"You didn't." The only time Joanna disobeyed Greta was when Greta told her to alter the timing of her menstrual cycle because, according to Greta, it should have come in the middle of the week instead of at the end.

Age 15 Running the Streets of LA

Greta and her gang, comprised largely of her loyal dodtees, Joanna, Brenda, and several other girls from Beverly Hills ran the streets of Los Angeles. Their wealth and contacts provided weapons and training at warfare. Joanna's ability to hack into their 'enemies' web sites, provided knowledge about meetings, battles, and financial information about those enemies largely female gangs. Largely most of those gangs were African American, Latina, and Asian. None were from Beverly Hills, from wealthy and influential families, and primarily American. Nor had any of them possess at that time, the hacking skills of Joanna.

The Bi'hes waged war with the other female gangs and a few of the male gangs who totally underestimated the warfare skills of the Bi'hes patricianly the criminally violent skills of their leader – Greta. For the most part, The Bi'hes smuggled in their own cocaine and heroin and relied on no one other than their sources for protection and supplies. In the summer months, the Bi'hes were outselling the Armenian Power, the Nazi Lowriders, and the Sons of Samoa all male gangs and they cut them physically and with force from their buying and selling drug territories. Many of the gang members did not like being replaced by "bitches." They went after the gang and much to their shock, their members were badly beaten and lost 'face' in LA.

At 16 Incarceration as Serial Killer

Other gangs such as the Black Guerrilla Family, the Triads, and the 18th Street gang sent emissaries toward peace treaties with the Bi'hes. Joanna was the lead discussant during those meetings which ended well for all concerned. Greta sat at a distance observing the transactions between those emissaries and Joanna, but one guess was that she was evaluating her prey. A week or so after one of those meetings, she attacked three Triad gang members including their emissary, killing two of them until SWAT officers had her surrounded. She attacked one of the officers and killed her in a few short moments. She was arrested, tried and convicted of serial murder since the prosecution was able to charge her with other unsolved murders. Her family totally backed off not wanting any publicity. She accepted a guilty plea in lieu of capital punishment and received life in prison without parole. She was sent to the Department of Corrections for security assignment which wasn't hard to determine. She was sent to a male prison because she was born male, but she was a high risk and had to be isolated, handcuffed, and angle bracelets at all times. Despite the precautions, she attacked two correctional officers during cell inspection harming both of the enough to send one to the morgue and one the hospital. The officer at the hospital told those taking his statement that he heard a loud scream coming from the ceiling and looking up for its source, the next thing was that he was on the ground and the prisoner was chewing at the neck of his partner. "It was a horrible sight. Here was a person totally restricted and yet the mouth of the prisoner appeared like that of a wild thing. Jumping toward me with parts of my partner's neck veins in her month, I shivered. Fortunately, the video in the cell alerted others and they said it took four COs to pull that monster from me. She savagely bit two of them, but hey I'm alive thanks to them. It's strange, though, I wasn't the first officer in her cell, but when she saw me, she stopped with them and attacked me. Maybe she knew that I wanted to kill her. Instincts, hahh? She's an animal not a human."

Update

Greta was eventually brutally killed by a sister of one of her victims when Greta was on the streets. The sister was a correctional captain and learned from Greta's other encounters with the correctional staff that it would prove helpful to leave her restraints in place while Greta was in the yard for her 30 minutes of fresh air. Then, drug her, and kill her. They blamed Greta's murder on a deranged prisoner in the yard at the time. For some reason the video of the yard went blank during the murder.

1 Amy Morin. (2020). Signs of Psychopathy in Kids. verywellfamily. Retrieved From https://www.verywellfamily.com/is-my-child-a-psychopath-4175470

2 Susan Krauss Whitbourne. (2016). Can We Identify Psychopathy in a Young Child? Psychology Today. Retrieved From https://www.psychologytoday.com/us/blog/fulfillment-any-age/201611/can-we-identify-psychopathy-in-young-child

3 Quote Investigator. (2012). Some People Feel the Rain. Others Just Get Wet. Retrieved From https://quoteinvestigator.com/2012/09/21/get-wet/

4 David Rodemerk. (2018). Predator Theory: The Ultimate Predator Has Schwarzenegger's DNA. ScreenRant. Retrieved From https://screenrant.com/predator-movie-theory-schwarzenegger-dna/

5 Stanton E. Samenow. (2014). Inside the Criminal Mind, Revised. New York: Broadway Books (pages 14-20). Also see Nicole Rafter. (2008). The Criminal Brain. New York: New York University Press (pages 1-4, 239).

6 James Alan Fox and Jack Levin. (2014). Extreme Killing: Understanding Serial and Mass Murder, 3rd Edition. New York: Sage Publications.

7 Eric W. Hickey. (2015). Serial Murderers and Their Victims. Boston: Cengage Learning. Retrieved From https://www.washingtonpost.com/local/public-safety/he-delivered-their-babies-and-examined-their-bodies-now-patients-are-suing-after-learning-he-used-a-fake-name-and-stolen-social-security-numbers-for-credentials/2017/12/30/b2732232-e43a-11e7-ab50-621fe0588340_story.html

8 Steven Rich, Ted Mellnik, Kimbriell Kelly & Wesley Lowery. (2018). Murder With Impunity. Washington Post. Retrieved From https://www.washingtonpost.com/graphics/2018/investigations/unsolved-homicide-database/

9 FBI. (2019). Uniform Crime Report. Retrieved From https://ucr.fbi.gov/crime-in-the-u.s/2018/crime-in-the-u.s.-

2018/topic-pages/tables/table-25

[10] District Attorney: County of Los Angeles. (2020). Criminal Elements. Retrieved From https://courses.lumenlearning.com/suny-criminallaw/chapter/4-1-criminal-elements/

[11] Rod Gehl & Darryl Piecas. (2017). Introduction to Criminal Investigation: Processes, Practices and Thinking. Chapter 3 Justice Institute of British Columbia. Retrieved From https://pressbooks.bccampus.ca/criminalinvestigation/chapter/chapter-3-what-you-need-to-know-about-evidence/

[12] Staff Writers. (2020). Alleged fraudulent COVID-19 treatments spark FBI raid of Shelby Twp medical spa. Fox 2 Detroit. Retrieved From https://www.fox2detroit.com/news/alleged-fraudulent-covid-19-treatments-spark-fbi-raid-of-shelby-twp-medical-spa

[13] Ames Alexander and Dan Kane. (2020). Coronavirus cases surge at NC women's prison. The Charlotte Observer. Retrieved From https://www.charlotteobserver.com/news/coronavirus/article242314121.html

[14] Christopher Buchanan and Andy Pierrotti. (2018). Georgia teacher who fired gun in classroom had previous, bizarre run-ins with police. USAToday. Retrieved From https://www.usatoday.com/story/news/nation-now/2018/03/01/georgia-teacher-bizarre-police-run-ins/384164002/

[15] Pauli Poisuo. (2020). The Most Dangerous Active Serial Killers. Grunge. Retrieved From https://www.grunge.com/200167/the-most-dangerous-active-serial-killers-in-2020/?utm_campaign=clip

[16] Mark Oliver. (2019). 23 Of History's Most Ruthless Female Serial Killers. Retrieved From https://allthatsinteresting.com/female-serial-killers

[17] Comprised of 140 Tibetan homes, each with a distinctive crown-shaped roof, red eaves and white walls. They are scattered among winding brooks like the pieces of a chessboard, with the occasional kitchen chimney puffing up smoke from a wood fire. Grove upon grove of apple and pear trees are everywhere. Emerald terraced fields stand in stark contrast to severe mountain heights and white snow peaks. Source: China Highlights. (2020). Jiaju Tibetan

Village. Retrieved From
https://www.chinahighlights.com/ganzi/attraction/jiaju-tibetan-
village.htm

[18] China Highlights. (2 The Hong Kong College of Orthopaedic
Surgeons 018). Jiaju Tibetan Village. Retrieved From
https://www.chinahighlights.com/ganzi/attraction/jiaju-tibetan-
village.htm

[19] Editors at Large. (2012). Buddhism Religion: Basic Beliefs and
Practices. Columbia Encyclopedia Retrieved From
https://www.infoplease.com/encyclopedia/religion/eastern/buddhis
m/buddhism/basic-beliefs-and-practices

[20] Starbucks has over 4,200 stores in 177cities in mainland China,
employing over 57,000 personnel. Source: Starbucks in China.
Retrieved From https://www.starbucks.com.cn/en/about/

[21] Robert Foyle Hunwick. (2017). Big in China: Murder Villages and
Scam Towns. In some rural areas, crime has become a cottage
industry. The Atlanta. Retrieved From
https://www.theatlantic.com/magazine/archive/2017/04/big-in-
china-murder-villages-and-scam-towns/517809/

[22] Andrew Jacobs. (2014). Tibetan Woman Dies After Setting
Herself on Fire in China. New York Times. Retrieved From
https://www.nytimes.com/2014/12/24/world/asia/tibetan-woman-
dies-after-setting-herself-on-fire-in-china.html

[23] ABC News. (2018). The fake doctors who get away with medical
fraud - ABC News. Retrieved From
https://www.abc.net.au/news/2018-04-10/fake-doctors-medical-
fraud/9634674

[24] Marina del Rey Hospital. (2020). What are the most common
orthopedic surgeries? Retrieved From
https://www.marinahospital.com/faq/what-are-the-most-common-
orthopedic-surgeries

[25] Stephanie Pagones. (2020). Drug trafficking 'completely disrupted'
by coronavirus pandemic: DEA
Prices for marijuana spiked by 55% since March. FoxBusiness.
Retrieved From https://www.foxbusiness.com/lifestyle/drug-
trafficking-completely-disrupted-by-coronavirus-pandemic-dea-

head

[26] PIT. (2019). Chinese man arrested at Delhi airport for smuggling anti-cancer medicine worth Rs 1.23 crore. Retrieved From https://health.economictimes.indiatimes.com/news/industry/chines e-man-arrested-at-delhi-airport-for-smuggling-anti-cancer-medicine-worth-rs-1-23-crore/68278561

[27] American Council of Science and Health. (2020). How To Spot A Fake Doctor. Retrieved From https://www.acsh.org/news/2019/02/13/how-spot-fake-doctor-13812

[28] O. Dyer. (2018). Six US doctors are charged in $464m opioid and fake treatment scheme. BMJ, 363:k5259. doi:10.1136/bmj.k5259

[29] Allister Hagger. (2009). Fake surgeon who operated 190 times. Express.co.uk. Retrieved From https://www.express.co.uk/news/uk/132700/Fake-surgeon-who-operated-190-times

[30] Becky Little. High-Ranking Viking Warrior Long Assumed to Be Male Was Actually Female. History.com. Retrieved Fromhttps://www.history.com/news/viking-warrior-female-gender-identity

[31] Culture Trip. (2020). The 10 Most Dangerous Cities in The World. Retrieved From https://theculturetrip.com/asia/pakistan/articles/the-10-most-dangerous-cities-in-the-world/

[32] Anushay Hossain. (2020). Massacre at maternity ward shows a chilling truth for women in Afghanistan. CNNews. Retrieved From https://www.cnn.com/2020/05/14/opinions/afghanistan-maternity-ward-massacre-hossain/index.html

[33] Rod Nordland. (2017). 11-Year-Old Has Spent Her Life in Jail, a Serial Killer as a Cellmate. New York Times. Retrieved From https://www.nytimes.com/2017/12/03/world/asia/afghanistan-children-prison.html?auth=link-dismiss-google1tap

[34] Rod Nordland. (2017). 11-Year-Old Has Spent Her Life in Jail, a Serial Killer as a Cellmate. New York Times. Retrieved From https://www.nytimes.com/2017/12/03/world/asia/afghanistan-children-prison.html?auth=link-dismiss-google1tap

[35] Editors of London-inter-faith. (2013). Verses on Satan. Retrieved

From http://londoninterfaith.org.uk/dirwp/wp-content/uploads/2013/09/Satan-Muslim-texts.pdf

[36] BBC. (2020). Salat: daily prayers. Retrieved From https://www.bbc.co.uk/religion/religions/islam/practices/salat.shtml

[37] God ordered Muslims to pray at five set times of day. Source see endnote 5
- Salat al-fajr: dawn, before sunrise
- Salat al-zuhr: midday, after the sun passes its highest
- Salat al-'asr: the late part of the afternoon
- Salat al-maghrib: just after sunset
- Salat al-'isha: between sunset and midnight

[38] Stan Grant. (2014). Kids learn hate at Afghan mosque. CNNews. Retrieved From http://www.cnn.com/2011/WORLD/asiapcf/05/11/afghanistan.madrassa/index.html

[39] Afghan Child Education and Care Organization (AFCECO), (2020).About AFCECO. Retrieved From https://afceco.org/index.php/programs/how-we-are/aboutus

[40] Luke Mogelson. (2019). The Shattered Afghan Dream of Peace. The New Yorker. Retrieved From https://www.newyorker.com/magazine/2019/10/28/the-shattered-afghan-dream-of-peace

[41] Bahaar Joya. (2017). Afghan Women Fight for Their Identity With #WhereIsMyName. Global Citizen. Retrieved From Afghan Women Fight for Their Identity With #WhereIsMyName

[42] United Religions Initiative. (2020). Islam: Basic Beliefs. Retrieved From https://uri.org/kids/world-religions/muslim-beliefs

[43] Tela Goodwin. (2019). Women in "witch cult" take stand, tell of control, promises of power from killing. FOX42. Retrieved From https://fox42kptm.com/news/local/woman-continues-testimony-in-trail-trial-talks-about-being-controlled-tortured

[44] Martin Kuz. (2016). Weary soldiers battling ghosts in Afghanistan. San Antonio Express News. Retrieved From https://www.expressnews.com/news/local/article/Weary-soldiers-battling-ghosts-in-Afghanistan-10625577.php

[45] Luke Mogelson. (2019). The Shattered Afghan Dream of Peace. The New Yorker. Retrieved From https://www.newyorker.com/magazine/2019/10/28/the-shattered-

afghan-dream-of-peace

[46] Holly Yan. (2014). Insider attacks: why do some Afghan forces turn and kill allies? CNNews. Retrieved From https://www.cnn.com/2014/08/06/world/asia/afghanistan-insider-attacks/index.html

[47] Charlie Savage, Eric Schmitt & Michael Schwirtz. (2020). Russia Secretly Offered Afghan Militants Bounties to Kill U.S. Troops, Intelligence Says. New York Times. Retrieved From https://www.nytimes.com/2020/06/26/us/politics/russia-afghanistan-bounties.html

[48] Damascus University. (2020). School of Medicine. Retrieved From http://damascusuniversity.edu.sy/med/

[49] BBC News. (2016). Syria: The Story of the conflict. Retrieved From https://www.bbc.com/news/world-middle-east-26116868

[50] Al-Fanar Media Reporting Team. (2017). The Difficulty of Studying Medicine in Times of War. Newsdeeply. Retrieved From https://www.newsdeeply.com/syria/articles/2017/10/30/the-difficulty-of-studying-medicine-in-times-of-war

[51] Pathfinders. (2020). Our Services. Retrieved From https://www.pathfindersmke.org/our-services/

[52] Jack Guy. (2019). Thirteen police killed in Mexico cartel ambush. CNNEWS. Retrieved From https://www.cnn.com/2019/10/15/americas/mexico-police-ambush-scli-intl/index.html

[53] Jane Flowers. (2019). Mother had sex with rapist killer of her 10-year-old daughter; says she enjoyed it. Blastingnews. Retrieved From https://us.blastingnews.com/news/2016/10/mother-had-sex-with-rapist-killer-of-her-10-year-old-daughter-says-she-enjoyed-it-001178363.html

[54] Meghan Leahy. (2019). Our 6-year-old's meltdowns are taking over our family. Washington Post. Retrieved From https://www.washingtonpost.com/lifestyle/on-parenting/our-6-year-olds-meltdowns-are-taking-over-our-family/2019/02/11/1e9b329c-2a49-11e9-b011-d8500644dc98_story.html

[55] WLTX. (2020). Death of missing SC 6-year-old Faye Swetlik under investigation. Retrieved From https://www.wltx.com/article/news/local/faye-swetlik-found-

dead/101-54dae187-9083-45df-870e-d63d7b55e6c3

[56] xKitty Crunchx. (2016). How to summon: slenderman. Retrieved From https://www.wattpad.com/135190042-summoning-the-creepypastas-how-to-summon. Summoning the creepypastas - ...www.wattpad.com › 13519004

[57] Creepypasta. (2020). Retrieved From https://www.creepypasta.com/

[58] Crime Investigation. (2020). Six Notorious Child Criminals. Crime Investigation. Retrieved From https://www.crimeandinvestigation.co.uk/article/six-notorious-child-criminals

[59] U.S. Department of Justice. (2020). U.S. Army Soldier Sentenced to Life in Prison for Aggravated Sexual Assault. Retrieved From https://www.justice.gov/opa/pr/us-army-soldier-sentenced-life-prison-aggravated-sexual-assault

[60] Heidi Poole. (2016). Girl Killer: True Stories of Teen Girls Who Kill. NY: CreateSpace Independent Publishing Platform.

[61] La Boheme UK Ltd. (2020). Absinthe Drink - Absinthe Liquor with Wormwood, How 2 Drink. Retrieved From https://www.originalabsinthe.com/buy-real-absinthe-online

[62] Jesse Hicks (2010, 2020). The Devil in a Little Green Bottle: A History of Absinthe. Science History Institute. Retrieved From

[63] Dean Hawley & Candace Heisler. (2012). Strangulation and Suffocation. NAPSA Conference 2012. Retrieved From http://www.napsa-now.org/wp-content/uploads/2012/11/102.pdf

[64] Richard Chiu. (2016). How long would it take for a person to die of strangulation? Quora. Retrieved From https://www.quora.com/How-long-would-it-take-for-a-person-to-die-of-strangulation

[65] Steve Myall & Suchandrika Chakrabarti. (2019).Children who kill - From shootings to stranglings, 12 evil kids and how they took another young life. Mirror. Retrieved From https://www.mirror.co.uk/news/world-news/kids-who-kill-shootings-stranglings-8753436

[66] Sam Meehan. (2018). Can you kill someone with a wire? Quora. Retrieved From https://www.quora.com/Can-you-kill-someone-with-a-wire

[67] Mayo Clinic Staff. (2020). Children's Health. Mayo Clinic. Retrieved From https://www.mayoclinic.org/healthy-

lifestyle/childrens-health/in-depth/mental-illness-in-children/art-20046577

[68] Human Rights Watch. (ND). The Odyssey of a Russian Orphan. Human Rights Watch. Retrieved From https://www.hrw.org/legacy/reports98/russia2/Russ98d-03.htm

[69] Mayo Clinic Staff. (2020). Children's Health. Mayo Clinic. Retrieved From https://www.mayoclinic.org/healthy-lifestyle/childrens-health/in-depth/mental-illness-in-children/art-20046577

[70] Jenny Gold. (2012). Women's Health in Juvenile Detention: How a System Designed for Boys Is Failing Girls. The Atlantic. Retrieved From https://www.theatlantic.com/health/archive/2012/11/womens-health-in-juvenile-detention-how-a-system-designed-for-boys-is-failing-girls/265668/

[71] Editors. (ND). What has allowed genocide to occur in Guatemala, and how can we guard against it happening again? New Mexico University. Retrieved From https://www.nmu.edu/english/sites/DrupalEnglish/files/UserFiles/WritingAwards/Cohodas/genocide_in_Guatemala.pdf

[72] Pauli Poisuo. (2020). PEDRO ALONZO LOPEZ may have killed over 300 people. Grunge. Retrieved From https://www.grunge.com/200167/the-most-dangerous-active-serial-killers-in-2020/

[73] Al Argueta. (2020). Religion in Guatemala: Mayan Spirituality, Catholicism, and Christianity. Hachette Book Group. Retrieved From https://www.hachettebookgroup.com/travel/arts-culture/religion-in-guatemala-mayan-spirituality-catholicism-and-christianity/

[74] Maria C. Gomez. (2020). Mayan Religion. Ancient History Encyclopedia. Retrieved From

[75] Walwyn. (2018). Devil & Nun, Chartres Cathedral. Ancient History Encyclopedia. Retrieved From https://www.ancient.eu/image/9322/

[76] Encyclopedia.com. (2020). Mayan Genocide In Guatemala. Retrieved From https://www.encyclopedia.com/social-sciences/encyclopedias-almanacs-transcripts-and-maps/mayan-genocide-guatemala

[77] Casey Grover & Reb Close. (2018). The Holy Trinity. The

Monterey County Prescribe Safe Initiative. Retrieved From https://www.chomp.org/app/files/public/7489/Holy-Trinity-article.pdf

[78] Madeline Drexler. (2011). Life after death: Helping former child soldiers become whole again. Harvard T.H. Chan. Retrieved From https://www.hsph.harvard.edu/news/magazine/child-soldiers-betancourt/

[79] K. Thor Jensen. (2016). The Insane History Of Female Demons. OMC Facts. Retrieved From https://medium.com/omgfacts/the-insane-history-of-female-demons-b2ced340c913

[80] Transcendental Meditation. (2015). The super powers of meditation: Are you ready to become a supernatural being? Retrieved From https://tmhome.com/benefits/10-superpowers-you-will-get-when-meditating/

[81] Fandom. (2020). Witches of East End Wiki. Retrieved From https://witchesofeastend.fandom.com/wiki/Mind_Control

[82] April A Taylor. (2018). Serial Killers Who Were Murdered By Their Last Targeted Victims. Ranker, Unspeakable Times. Retrieved From https://www.ranker.com/list/serial-killers-killed-by-victims/april-a-taylor

[83] Abhishek Ranjan. (2020). Cyber Criminals and its types. GeeksforGeeks. Retrieved From https://www.geeksforgeeks.org/cyber-criminals-and-its-types/

[84] Toretto. (2020). Brute Force Attack. GeeksforGeeks. Retrieved From https://www.geeksforgeeks.org/brute-force-attack/?ref=leftbar-rightbar

[85] MedlinePlus. (2020). Mental Disorders. Retrieved From https://medlineplus.gov/mentaldisorders.html

[86] Chris McCrory. (2020). 27 people have been killed in New Orleans through two months in 2020. Retrieved From https://www.wwltv.com/article/news/crime/27-people-have-been-killed-in-new-orleans-this-year-all-but-one-were-shot-to-death/289-1d5b5a93-f08e-45fa-b0ec-fa27c493326c

[87] Mayo Clinic. (2020). Panic attacks and panic disorder. Retrieved From https://www.mayoclinic.org/diseases-conditions/panic-attacks/symptoms-causes/syc-20376021

[88] Heidi Poole. (2016). Girl Killer: True Stories of Teen Girls Who Kill. NY: CreateSpace Independent Publishing Platform.

[89] Rachel E Kahn, Amy L Byrd, & Dustin A. Pardini. (2012). Callous-unemotional traits robustly predict future criminal offending in young men. Law Hum Behavior. 2013 Oct;37(5):376]. Law Human Behavior. 2013;37(2):87-97. doi:10.1037/b0000003

Made in the USA
Columbia, SC
17 January 2023

75505566R00131